The Exiles in Love

HILARY McKAY

The Exiles in Love

MARGARET K. McELDERRY BOOKS

Margaret K. McElderry Books
An imprint of Simon & Schuster Children's Publishing Division
1230 Avenue of the Americas
New York, NY 10020

Book design by Michael Nelson
The text of this book was set in Goudy.

Printed in the United States of America
10 9 8 7 6 5 4 3 2

Library of Congress Cataloging-in-Publication Data
McKay, Hilary.
The exiles in love / Hilary McKay.—1st U.S. ed.
p.   cm.
Summary: When Big Grandma takes the four Conroy sisters on holiday as a cure for the
"family failing," the girls wonder if their grandmother herself is still susceptible to it.
ISBN 0-689-81752-5
[1. Sisters—Fiction. 2. Grandmothers—Fiction. 3. England—Fiction.] I. Title.
PZ7.M4786574Ey   1998
[Fic]—dc21
97-30237
CIP   AC

*T*o everyone who asked what happened next

Chapter One

"YOU STARTED ALL THIS, you know!"

"Me?"

"That first spring when we all fell in love."

"Begin at the beginning; how old were we?"

"You were nearly fifteen, so I must have been thirteen and a half, a bit young for the family failing to strike!"

"Rachel was even younger. She was only ten."

"But it started with you."

"It started with the hedgehog."

Ruth was the eldest of the Conroy girls. In a few weeks' time she would be fifteen.

"I used to think that fifteen would be nearly grown up," said her sister Naomi, "until you started being it."

Ruth knew exactly what she meant; she had felt the same way herself and she thought the strangest thing about being so old was the fact that it made no difference at all. She was no more self-confident, or organized, or magically in charge of her emotions than she had been in the past. Nothing had changed; she was the same muddle-headed person she had always been, forever swinging between happiness and despair, never doing the right thing at quite the right moment. Naomi, eighteen months younger and two years behind her at school, had far more common sense.

Naomi was brainy, and a much more private person than Ruth. While Ruth either dreamed of miracles or expected the worst, Naomi took a more detached view of life. She and Ruth were very good allies; they understood each other. They read the same books, liked the same friends, detested the same enemies, and managed to share a bedroom and yet remain on speaking terms most of the time. They endured with courage their little sisters Rachel and Phoebe.

"Although they really are not sane," remarked Ruth gloomily.

"Don't be silly!" said her mother, although secretly thinking that Ruth had a point. "Phoebe has been at the top of her class since the day she started school!"

"That's got nothing to do with whether she's bonkers or not," observed Naomi.

"And Rachel's teacher says she is a 'good average,'" continued Mrs. Conroy. "And should be encouraged."

Rachel was ten. Her latest preoccupation was What They Ate in Books. She had dreams of munching her way through literature.

"After all, it's really quite original!" said Mrs. Reed, Rachel's class teacher, when Mrs. Conroy came to see her at the annual parents' evening. "And it can't be easy for her. All those clever sisters, including Phoebe coming on behind!"

Mrs. Conroy sighed rather ruefully. "I wish I had normal daughters," she remarked.

"*Of course* you have normal daughters!" exclaimed Mrs. Reed with a dreadful false brightness.

"I should never have taught them to read so early."

"Early reading is an absolutely *splendid* achievement!" Mrs. Reed assured her. "Absolutely *splendid!* Dramatically broadens their horizons!"

Mrs. Conroy went home and looked at her daughters. Their horizons seemed dramatically narrow. There was Ruth, dripping with tears over *Little Women* (which she must have read a hundred times before). There was Naomi, droning aloud snatches of the poems of Housman.

"I'm sure they're not suitable for a girl of thirteen," protested Mrs. Conroy.

"Thirteen and a half," said Naomi, "and we did the 'cherry hung with snow' one in English literature before the teacher ran away with the French assistant. Listen!" And she read aloud with great enjoyment:

> "*Before this fire of sense decay,*
> *This smoke of thought blow clean away,*
> *And leave with ancient night alone,*
> *The steadfast and enduring bone.*"

"Very morbid and exaggerated and I'm sure you can't understand a word of it!" said Mrs. Conroy, and turned away, and there was Phoebe, who at the age of eight read nothing but spy stories obtained by devious means from the adult library.

Last of all, there was Rachel.

"*Not* bonkers!" Mrs. Conroy told herself firmly.

"What's sow belly?" asked Rachel, looking up from her book. "They seem to eat a lot of it in America. How was the parents' evening? Did Mrs. Reed say nice things about me?"

"Why ever shouldn't she?" asked Mrs. Conroy evasively.

Rachel and Phoebe both went to the same junior school. Ruth and Naomi attended the local comprehensive, traveling back and forth by school bus. It was just on the point of leaving the school one April afternoon when Ruth, tearstained, disheveled, and breathless, scrabbled aboard.

"Don't tell me you've had cooking today *again*," remarked Naomi as Ruth flopped down beside her, and she regarded her sister's wicker cooking basket with suspicion and disgust. "We've only just gotten through eating the last lot."

Ruth did not reply. She sat silently clutching her basket, hunched against the motion of the bus.

"If it's more meat loaves," said Naomi, "I can't bear it. I shall turn vegetarian like Phoebe."

Waste not, want not was a very firm policy in the Conroy household. If it was food, it was eaten, and that was that. So far the results of Ruth's cooking lessons had been counted as food.

"No one could eat them," continued Naomi. "I don't

know why you had to bring them home!"

"They were turkey rissoles," said Ruth defensively, "and Rachel ate them."

Naomi snorted with derision, and several people who had been listening laughed out loud. Ruth held her basket even more tightly and began to fumble around in her blazer pocket for something to wipe her nose on. While her sister was distracted Naomi raised a corner of the basket's plastic cover, peered inside, and then jumped back in alarm.

"What on earth is it?" she demanded. "It looks like a squashed hedgehog!"

"Leave it alone!" snapped Ruth.

"It was Simple Cottage Rolls today," someone from Ruth's class told Naomi helpfully.

The smell that had arisen from Ruth's basket when Naomi lifted the cover was not that of simple cottage rolls. It was a sweetish, rankish, rancidish smell. A hedgehoggy smell.

"Let me look again," said Naomi. "Let me look properly. It's only fair if I've got to eat it."

Ruth gave in. After all, Naomi would have to know sometime or other. Gently she uncovered the contents of her basket enough to allow Naomi to look again.

It was a squashed hedgehog.

"Don't frighten it," said Ruth.

"Isn't it dead, then?"

"Of course not. It's just curled up. But a car's hit it; there's blood on some of its spines. I found it in the gutter by the school gates."

"When?"

"Afternoon break."

"Where's it been since then?"

"In my cooking basket."

"What did you do with the rolls you made, then?"

"Chucked them away."

"Well, that's something," said Naomi with relief.

The whole bus had been quiet while people eavesdropped on this conversation, but now the silence erupted into a torrent of noise. Squashed hedgehog jokes were called from seat to seat, and there were loud predictions about the agility and appetite of the invalid's fleas. Ruth was assailed by shouts of advice, compliments on the sudden improvement of her culinary skills, squeals of disgust, and wailings of sympathy. Egg Yolk Wendy, the girl who always knew everything, hung over the back of the seat to tell her the name of a vet to whom she herself had once taken a squashed hedgehog.

"He did it for me free," she said.

"Did what?" demanded Naomi.

"Put it to sleep."

"Ought you to have wrapped it in your sweater?" asked Martin-the-Good, leaning across the aisle to peer over Ruth's shoulder.

"Anyone started itching yet?" inquired a voice from the back of the bus, and was answered by shrieks and hoots from all sides. Two people fell scratching and writhing into the aisle. The noise reached a crescendo. Ruth, unable to bear it any longer, thrust the basket into Naomi's arms, and was preparing to leap to her feet and do battle when everyone suddenly cannoned forward as the bus jerked to a halt.

"ENOUGH!" roared the driver, blasting his passengers into silence. "PACK IT IN!"

Rescued, limp with astonishment and relief, Ruth stared at him in admiration. No knight in shining armor could ever have made a more efficient or welcome rescue.

"Crikey!" said the bus driver in an ordinary voice, and drove on.

Once Ruth was off the bus, the reactions to the contents of her cooking basket were slightly better.

"Ought you to have wrapped it in your sweater?" asked Mrs. Collingwood, the Conroys' next-door neighbor and mother of Martin-the-Good, but she added, "Poor little thing!"

"You ought *not* to have wrapped it in your sweater!" said Ruth's mother. "Still, I suppose it will wash. Put it in the shed and leave it in peace and we'll see how it is after supper."

"Gypsies used to eat hedgehogs," remarked Rachel through a mouthful of macaroni and cheese. "Covered in mud and baked in their jackets."

"Shut up!" said Ruth.

"I think that's cruel," continued Rachel. "Their poor little prickles cooking!"

"Shut *up!*" ordered Ruth.

"No worse than eating sheep," Phoebe pointed out. "Or cows. Or pigs. Or horses."

"I *don't* eat horses," protested Rachel.

"They do in France," said Phoebe. "I expect you would if you were there."

❧ ❧ ❧

After supper there was a worried hedgehog inspection.

"It will have to see a vet," said Ruth at last. "How much do you think it will cost?"

"Wendy said it was free."

"That was just for putting it down. I want to make this one better."

"Ask when you telephone," suggested Naomi.

Unfortunately when Ruth telephoned she found that the nearest veterinary office was closed for the day. So was the next nearest. So was the next nearest to that, which was twelve miles away and not near at all. Ruth left messages on all three answering machines, describing (with sobs) the extremeness of the emergency, but carefully not mentioning the species of animal involved. This was a precaution in case a hedgehog wouldn't be considered important enough to deserve an after-hours visit.

"Don't you think it's a bit much," asked Naomi, "calling out three vets to one squashed hedgehog? What will Mum say if they all turn up together in the middle of the night?"

"What else could I do?" asked Ruth. "She'll know I had to. She won't mind."

"I bet she will."

"I'll find out," said Rachel, and before she could be stopped had dashed into the kitchen. A moment later they could hear her breathlessly inquiring, "Do you mind that Ruth has telephoned three midnight vets to come and see her hedgehog?"

"What *do* you mean?"

"She told them on their answering machines that it was life or death. She said you wouldn't mind."

"Ruth! You couldn't have been so silly!" exclaimed Mrs. Conroy, hurrying out of the kitchen.

"Why is it silly?" asked Ruth, still sniffing. "What else could I do?"

"Sometimes," said Mrs. Conroy crossly, "you behave more like four than fourteen! For goodness' sake go and look up their numbers and cancel them, Naomi! Rachel, I saw you! Come out of that cupboard! You've had your supper! And where has Phoebe vanished to just at bedtime?"

"She's gone next door," said Rachel through a handful of hastily purloined raisins. "Practicing her spying, I expect."

"You girls go from one silly phase to another!" said Mrs. Conroy. "Go and fetch her, someone, and apologize to Mrs. Collingwood if she's been rude . . . *not* you, Rachel!"

But Rachel had already gone, furtively chewing desiccated coconut as she went. She liked Mrs. Collingwood, who always asked if she was hungry, and Martin-the-Good (who she was planning to marry if the worst came to the worst), and Martin's little brother, Peter, who saved his cookie crumbs and sandwich corners for her, and Josh, the next-door dog, and most of all she liked apologizing for her sisters, especially Phoebe, who was often difficult to keep squashed into her proper place as the youngest of the family.

"Mum says she's sorry if Phoebe's been rude," she told Mrs. Collingwood smugly.

"Rude?" asked Mrs. Collingwood. "Phoebe?"

"Spying," explained Rachel.

"Spying!" Mrs. Collingwood laughed. "She's been unloading the dishwasher, good as gold!"

"Oh," said Rachel, very disappointed. "Well, anyway, it's her bedtime."

Phoebe said good night to the Collingwoods and went with Rachel very meekly, but on the street outside she remarked, "Do you know what happens to people who blow other people's cover?"

"What?" asked Rachel.

"I'll lend you a book," said Phoebe.

Naomi, who would not have chosen to sleep in the same room as a wounded, flea-ridden hedgehog, nevertheless recognized the inevitable and helped smuggle it upstairs for the night.

"And I didn't completely cancel those vets," she told Ruth. "I just gave them our number and said, 'It's a squashed hedgehog, actually, but it would be nice if you came.' But even if they don't, Mum says we can take it to the vet in the morning."

"It might be dead by morning," said Ruth gloomily. "It won't eat."

"And you gave the last hedgehog brandy, didn't you? I've sneaked the bottle up again."

"Thanks," said Ruth gratefully.

"But you'll have to take it down when you've finished. I'm going to bed."

Taking the brandy down was easy. Both Mr. and Mrs. Conroy were fully occupied with Rachel, who had struggled through enough of John le Carré to discover what happened to people who blew other people's cover. She wasn't getting much sympathy.

"If I've told you once, I've told you a thousand times, *stop calling Childline!*" Ruth heard Mrs. Conroy shout.

Late in the night Ruth jerked awake and lay listening. At first she heard nothing but Naomi's quiet breathing and the sound of the spring rain that was streaming down the windows outside. Then it came again: a little hollow ping, like the flick of a fingernail on a box.

Ruth knew that noise far too well; after all, it was not the first time a hedgehog had died under her bed. Those pings were produced by the fleas as they jumped from its cooling body and collided with the sides of the cardboard box. Ruth woke her sister to tell her the sad news, and it struck Naomi as funny.

"Don't you care that it's dead?" demanded Ruth.

"Of course I do," said Naomi. "But that noise always reminds me of popcorn. And, anyway, couldn't you have waited till morning to tell me?"

"Do you think it can possibly have gone to Heaven?"

This was Ruth's ritual question when confronted with death and Naomi was always firm.

"No," she said at once. "Because what would it do when it got there? Eat slugs and snails that had gone to Hell? It's just died, that's all. No good getting all drippy about it."

"Perhaps I shouldn't have given it that brandy."

"Brandy for shock," said Naomi. "Anyway, it's too late now."

"It didn't work on the last one either."

"Well, at least they die happy," murmured Naomi, and a moment later she was asleep.

Nobody cares, thought Ruth, as the tears soaked her pillow. *Those vets never came. Naomi thought it was funny. Mum was a lot more bothered about where Phoebe was and Rachel calling Childline. And they were horrible on the bus. Horrible. Horrible. Horrible.*

All at once she remembered what had stopped them being horrible.

"Did you notice the bus driver?" she asked Naomi, but her sister merely groaned.

He cared, thought Ruth. *He shut them up. It was brilliant the way he shut them up.* She wished she could remember more about him. Strange that she had seen him every school day for months and months and hardly noticed him before. Not that there had ever been much to notice. He was a silent young man, who usually only communicated by means of facial twitches, raised eyebrows, and rare loud shouts of despair addressed to nobody in particular and always uttered when the bus was in motion. Still, the fate of the hedgehog had not left him unmoved.

The pinging sounds from the box seemed endless.

I shall have to break it to the bus driver in the morning, thought Ruth, and sighed and fell asleep.

Morning came. In the corner of the Conroy garden reserved for such unfortunates (a rapidly expanding patch of pansies and gravestones), the hedgehog was buried. Ruth (between bites of toast) made a short but surprisingly optimistic speech committing his prickly soul to hedgehog heaven (where bread and milk were surely supplied to spare the feelings of the incumbent slugs and snails). Naomi found a piece of slate, wrote

on it, and erected it over the grave, while Rachel's suggestion that they "dig around a bit and see what's happened to the others" was dismissed as heartless and time-consuming. Phoebe watched the proceedings looking as solemn as an undertaker, making mental notes of all that went on as practice for her chosen career as an international spy.

"What does RIP stand for?" she inquired.

"Riddled in Parasites," Naomi told her, and the funeral degenerated into an invigorating fight. Ruth set off for the school bus in the highest of spirits and was totally unprepared for what followed. She climbed up the steps, all set to break the bad news that the hedgehog was dead and the good news that he was already successfully buried in a very pleasant spot, and found that she could not speak.

Nor could she move. Or think. She stood rooted, with Naomi and Martin standing impatiently behind her, while she stared idiotically into the bus driver's face. He had black curly hair and a slightly broken front tooth. He had a small star tattooed on one cheek.

He looked annoyed.

Ruth stood there.

He raised his eyes to Heaven and held out his hand. He had a bandage on his thumb and a heavy gold ring shaped like a snake. Ruth was conscious of a horrible hotness about her face and knew that she was blushing, a manifestation that usually only afflicted her when she told enormous, immediately detectable lies. Naomi poked her hard in the back and she realized they were all waiting for something.

"Pass?" snapped the driver.

Ruth nodded thankfully and stumbled to the nearest seat.

"PASS!" shouted the driver.

What is it? wondered Ruth. *Surely I am too young for a heart attack.*

"PASS!" yelled the driver again and Naomi pushed forward, took something from Ruth's unresisting fingers, and handed it back to him.

"Her hedgehog died," she told him, by way of explanation.

It seemed to Ruth that the world must have suddenly stopped spinning. Now it began again, and she found herself once more and knew what had happened.

I have fallen in love, she wrote, facing facts, in her diary that night. *With someone. The bus driver.* Written down it looked as stark as a death sentence. *He was nice about the hedgehog,* she continued, trying to soften the blow. *I don't know his name and I can't remember what he looks like. Except for a broken tooth. And a tattoo. And a ring. I have started reading* Jane Eyre, she added thankfully, sighing with relief to get onto familiar ground again. *Burned porridge is not half as bad as she makes out.*

It was terribly inconvenient, being in love with the bus

driver. Ruth had always found getting off to school each morning difficult enough as it was, and now it was much, much worse. It started with a dreadful feeling of numbness the moment she awoke, which gradually increased as the time approached when she must stand face-to-face with the object of her passion and hand over her bus pass. That was the point of extreme paralysis. It always seemed to go on for hours and only ended when Naomi shoved her in the back and made rude remarks from the step behind. Then, crimson-faced and with a pounding heart, Ruth would move forward and slowly begin to return to life. At the end of the day the whole nerve-racking process had to be gone through again. It seemed to Ruth that the words

IN LOVE WITH THE BUS DRIVER

must be painted across her forehead, and the only comfort was the fact that they were not.

Nobody around her, not even Naomi, appeared to have recognized her symptoms. Only the bus driver was slightly curious about her behavior.

"Some sort of punk revival is it, then?" he asked slightly wistfully on the second day of the affair.

"What?" asked Naomi, prodding her sister into a seat.

"This dead hedgehog thing?"

"Oh," said Naomi. "No. No, it was just a hedgehog that died under her bed, that's all. Sorry," she added, seeing the disappointment on the driver's face.

The bus driver shrugged his shoulders and went back to his long silences and Ruth escaped for a while with Jane

Eyre, who seemed to be as obsessed with food as her sister Rachel.

Nobody has guessed, she wrote in her diary that night. *I don't think. Although Egg Yolk Wendy did say in the middle of nothing that she thought he was feeling his age. The bus driver. You can get tattoos removed but it leaves scars. It says something else on his arm that I can't read. It is all upside down and hairy. Helen Burns is dying at Jane Eyre's school but Jane hasn't noticed.*

Jane Eyre soon stopped being such a comforting escape. Forty pages after she hadn't noticed the illness of poor Helen, Mr. Rochester arrived, tumbling from his horse at her undeserving feet and Ruth, still reeling from the effects of the school bus driver, was flattened again.

This is it again, she thought. *Two at once. I am a bigamist, or is it ambidextrous?* And she turned feverishly to the back of the book to read the end. There he was, burned, blind, and groveling to the unspeakable Jane. She ransacked the pages to see how this could possibly have come about and discovered the mad woman in the attic, Grace Pool the drunken nurse, and the money-grabbing Blanche. And poor majestic Mr. Rochester. Jane had abandoned him solely because he was unfortunate enough to possess a wife already. Here she was, pages and pages later, stealing cold porridge from the mouths of honest pigs.

"Ruth!" said Naomi urgently from behind. "RUTH! Wake up! Give him your bus pass!"

"Who?" asked Ruth vaguely. "Who?"

"The driver!" hissed Naomi.

Ruth fumbled her way out of her daze and back into life again. The bus driver gave her a stare of heart-melting indifference.

That was what it was like for Ruth, the first week of being in love. She gave up sleep in favor of Mr. Rochester's sardonic charms, and no sooner had morning arrived than the distant sound of diesel engines was blowing her mind.

Chapter Two

"RACHEL WANTED TO BE MAY QUEEN. Do you remember how she bathed her face in the dew?"

"I remember everything!"

"Mr. Blyton-Jones?"

"Agony!"

"Mortal. At the time."

"Phoebe was all right. No family failing for Phoebe!"

"Too busy being an international spy."

"Practicing on us! But it was Phoebe who started Rachel May Queening, you know. And look where it led to!"

"Yes, look!"

It was late spring: a time of miracles, dandelions on every patch of green, a rumor of frog-spawn in the ditches, and somebody had heard a cuckoo call. At Rachel and Phoebe's school plans for the celebration of May Day were in progress. A new May Queen would be appointed. Nominations were already being taken for the throne.

"Should you like it to be you?" Rachel asked Phoebe.

"No," said Phoebe.

"I should like it to be me," said Rachel.

Phoebe stared at her sister in surprise. Only for a few minutes in the morning did Rachel look presentable. Usually by the time she got downstairs she was beginning to come undone. For the rest of the day she looked as though she were falling apart, rather like a toy that has been played with by dozens of grubby children for years and years. Right now her hair was straggling in all directions from the remains of a fat brown braid, her clothes hung in grubby bunches, her nails were bitten, black-edged Band-Aids drooped from both knees, and she was walking with a curious, heaving gait, due to a large lump of chewing gum stuck on the sole of one shoe.

"Oh, I *should* like it to be me!" said Rachel wistfully.

"Would you really?"

"With a crown and a throne and wings."

"Not wings," said Phoebe firmly. "That's God. You're getting mixed up."

"Riding on a float around the playground."

"Milk-float," corrected Phoebe. "The Thin One's dad's milk-float."

"With flowers in my hair," continued Rachel, stooping to gather a bunch of fallen blossoms as they passed beneath a cherry tree.

"They're dead," said Phoebe.

"They're not. They're hardly trodden on. Does that look right? Or not?"

"Not," said Phoebe.

Rachel's smile turned upside down and she began to sniff.

"Put them a bit higher," said Phoebe, giving up, "then they will."

It was hard for Phoebe to be an international spy all the time; she was only eight years old and, despite her best efforts, every now and then her human side broke through. She had a system of dead-letter boxes in which she dropped occasional observations and speculations on life. The following day a new piece of information was added to the files.

Nominated Rachel for May Queen

recorded Phoebe (as usual not bothering to turn it into code because very few people could read her writing anyway). She heard Rachel's footsteps on the stairs just as she finished, and hurriedly posted it in her emergency dead-letter box, under a corner of the bedroom carpet.

Mrs. Conroy had known about the dead-letter boxes for some time, but had always nobly resisted the temptation to go through their contents. However, the May Queen intelligence almost disappeared inside the vacuum cleaner before she saw it; she caught it just in time and noticed Rachel's name at once.

Dear little Phoebe, she thought when she had smoothed it out and read its contents. *Dear little Phoebe; she is not all bad!*

And she replaced it carefully on the square of floorboards where Phoebe had written:

DEAD LETTER BOX

She is not bad at all! thought Mrs. Conroy, because this was exactly the way she had always dreamed of her daughters behaving.

"Like proper little girls," she told her mother when she telephoned her that night.

"Don't raise your hopes too high," warned Big Grandma. "Fond though I am of Rachel, she does not strike me as May Queen material. Far from it, I should say! But it's nice to know you're pleased with them. And while you're thinking positively . . ."

"I *must* do something about her hair."

"Cut it off!" said Big Grandma, who always thought everyone should have their hair chopped off. "You're not listening. I have an idea to put to you."

"I can't cut it off. She won't hear of it. She wants to grow it long enough to sit on!"

"Or dangle out the window," said Big Grandma. "They're growing up now! About time they acquired a bit of *je ne sais quoi*! And, speaking of which, do you remember those summers we spent in France when you were a child, after your father died?"

"We can't possibly afford to take the girls abroad this summer," said Mrs. Conroy in alarm.

"I know you can't. I wasn't going to suggest it. But do you remember Brittany? And the little stone house in Monsieur Carodoc's apple orchard?"

"Of course."

"And Julie Carodoc, who you played with? You know, we always kept in touch."

"You and Julie?"

"Monsieur Carodoc and I . . ."

"Really, Mother!" Mrs. Conroy exclaimed suddenly.

"Well, why ever shouldn't we have done? Charles and I were very good friends. I value my friends."

"Even so . . ."

"Do listen," said Big Grandma, so pleadingly that Mrs. Conroy did listen, only interrupting with such remarks as, "Impossible!" and, "As if I hadn't enough to do!" and, "Where could he possibly sleep?" All of which Big Grandma completely ignored.

"And how are Naomi and Ruth?" she asked, when Mrs. Conroy's last "Impossible!" seemed to have been uttered. "Have they followed Rachel and Phoebe's example? Are they also behaving like proper little girls at last?"

Mrs. Conroy was forced to admit that this was unfortunately not the case.

"Ruth has been dopier than ever since she brought home that last hedgehog that died under her bed," she told Big Grandma, "and I'm afraid Naomi has started writing poetry. As if reading it wasn't bad enough . . ."

"What is it like?"

"Very gloomy."

"Ah!" said Big Grandma ominously. "Well, think about my suggestion. Please. It would be so good for the girls."

"All very well!" began Mrs. Conroy.

"And mean such a lot to me."

❧ ❧ ❧

Darkest of trees, the bitter ash
Bows stricken by the lightning flash
And all about the woodland track
Fallen leaves are withered black.

Naomi had fallen in love. The Temporary English teacher had arrived.

He was straight from college, but as far as Naomi was concerned, he might have been straight from Mount Olympus. On his first morning he sauntered into the classroom, opened all the windows, and glanced contemptuously at the register.

"Had we but world enough, and time," he remarked, and tossed it to Naomi.

"Andrew Marvell," said Naomi, already completely lost to this dazzling combination of anarchy, poetry, and oxygen.

He stared at her in surprise. Surely she was a girl. She was certainly wearing a skirt. Perhaps this was one of those amazingly broad-minded schools one read about in the *Guardian*. (It certainly hadn't struck him that way at his interview.) Or perhaps he had hit upon a rebel already.

"Well, fill that in, then, er . . . Andrew," he replied cheerfully, and with that he pulled a book from his pocket, settled himself down on the teacher's desk with his feet resting on a nearby chair, and began to read aloud from *Henry V* (which was not in the curriculum).

It was an astonishing performance. Nobody in the class had ever heard anything like it before. And his voice was amazing; his audience (who, on hearing of his youth, had fondly expected to eat him alive) sat reeling while the words dropped like blows. It was like being forced to listen while someone banged an enormous gong over your head. When he stopped speaking they found there was still ringing in their ears.

"That's the bell," he said. "Off you pop. We live to fight another day. What did you think?"

There was no one left to answer except Naomi, who had just discovered that she had filled in the register with nobody absent until the end of term (which would certainly be the case if all his performances were as spectacular as his first).

"Trite," replied Naomi, to pay him back for thinking she was Andrew Marvell.

"Half-right," he said taking the register. "Trite but fantastic. You're not a boy, are you?"

"No," said Naomi.

Big Grandma telephoned again.

"Please," she said. "As a favor to me."

It was not like Big Grandma to ask for favors.

"Say yes," urged Mr. Conroy, when he and his wife discussed her suggestion that evening. "Why not? It's not as if you didn't know the family."

"A long time ago," remarked his wife.

"Not that long. And it's not often she asks for anything. And look at all she's done for our girls! Having them to stay. Taking them off to Africa!"

"Julie Carodoc was a nice girl," admitted Mrs. Conroy. "And those summers on the farm in France were lovely. I shall never forget them. Perhaps that's what she's remembering, too."

"What else could it be?" asked Mr. Conroy.

At school the Temporary English teacher continued to dumbfound his classes at full volume, reading aloud whatever he happened to grab from the English literature stockroom on his way up the stairs. Naomi's class was swept straight from Agincourt into the middle of a Cotswold winter, and no sooner had *Cider with Rosie* been gutted and slung back on the shelves than they were in Alabama, America, passionately not killing mockingbirds. And then, before they had time to catch breath, the cherry was once again being hung with snow. He had an unnerving habit of zigzagging backward and forward through the texts without bothering to explain his sudden leaps to his listeners, so they were left with a feeling of being hurled through a random assortment of time. Once, during a pause for breath, someone dared to ask, "What is it all about?"

"What is what all about?" asked the Temporary English teacher irritably.

"All this poetry and shouting and stuff."

"Stuff!" roared the Temporary English teacher. "It is your national heritage! English literature! And for homework tonight you can all of you write me a list of everything you have ever read. Stop groaning! I shall use it as a guide to your level of intelligence, so it had better be comprehensive. There's the bell. Go home. Has anyone filled in the register?"

"I filled it in last week," Naomi told him. "I filled all of us in till the end of the term."

"Have you second sight or something?"

"No," admitted Naomi, "but I expect we'll all be here."

"And do you wonder what it's all about?"

"Of course not," replied Naomi truthfully. She alone in the class had the advantage of already having read the contents of the English stockroom, and she said again, scornfully, "Of course not!"

The Temporary English teacher looked hard at Naomi. "You remind me of someone," he told her, and left the room.

At Rachel and Phoebe's school May Queen fever was heating up. The list of the ten people nominated for the throne was posted on the bulletin board outside the girls' bathroom. Luckily. Rachel read it, and it seemed as if the ground lurched beneath her feet. The hair on the back of her neck stood up, her skin became icy cold, she rushed into the bathroom and was sick.

On the way back outside she stole the list for herself.

It was the most momentous thing that had ever happened to her. It was like being offered a fresh start in a new life, a chance to be someone other than grubby, plodding Rachel, the girl with the three clever sisters. She pored over the list until it dropped to pieces in her warm, sticky hands, and she wondered constantly which discerning admirer had caused her to be included. It would have broken her heart to know that it was Phoebe. Fortunately Phoebe (although bored to howling point by the subject of

May Queens and already deeply regretting her moment of weakness) was not an international spy for nothing and could keep a secret.

"It means," said Rachel to Mrs. Conroy one morning, having struggled ferociously with statistics for half the night, "that I have a one in ten chance of being chosen. Doesn't it?"

"I suppose it must," admitted her mother.

"One in ten is quite high," continued Rachel. "If I had a one in ten chance of being squashed on the way to school like Ruth's hedgehog, would you let me go?"

"No," said Mrs. Conroy, not pausing in her daily ritual of straightening, mopping, and hitching Rachel into shape for the day.

"That's what I mean," said Rachel happily.

"If you really want to be chosen, you might try to keep looking nice," suggested Mrs. Conroy. "Clean and tidy."

Even as she spoke she knew that this was not possible, and that Rachel's permanent state of self-destruction was something beyond them both. It was as unstoppable as the gradual blackening of a banana, or radioactive decay. Rachel had long ago recognized this fact and made no attempt to save herself from her fate, but after the posting of the list outside the girls' bathroom she did make some effort to improve her appearance. Every morning, before setting off for school she visited the worn patch of grass that was Mr. Conroy's version of a lawn and bathed her face in the dew. Traditionally, she knew, this should be done before sunrise, but Rachel was not an early morning sort of person. So she bathed her face before school, and if the result was a little grassy and worm-casty and damp around the collar, it nevertheless shone with hope.

Observing for the first time this desperate behavior, Mrs. Conroy began to wonder if her mother was perhaps right in suggesting that a little *je ne sais quoi* would not come amiss with her daughters. She would have forbidden Rachel's beauty treatment altogether had she not suspected that if the aspiring May Queen was not allowed the use of the garden lawn dew, she would simply move her operations to another location, such as the grass plots by the pavements where people were in the habit of walking their dogs . . .

"Perhaps it wouldn't be a bad idea to do as Mother asks," she said to her husband. "At least it would be something to distract poor Rachel if the worst comes to the worst and she isn't chosen . . ."

"*When* the worst comes to the worst," corrected Mr. Conroy, who always believed in facing facts. "Go on! Telephone your mother and tell her yes."

"Yes," said Mrs. Conroy to Big Grandma.

"You are being very sensible! I am so glad!"

"But please don't tell the girls. I should like to save the news for a while. Something new to think about might be just what's needed when the May Queen results are announced."

"Or perhaps even sooner," said Big Grandma. "Is Naomi still persisting in writing poetry?"

"I'm afraid so," Mrs. Conroy admitted.

"And Ruth still wandering round in a daze? Do not forget the family failing. It goes back for centuries, even if it did skip a generation with you!"

"You and your family failings!" exclaimed Mrs. Conroy. "Absolute nonsense!"

"What is?" asked Phoebe, passing through the hall that moment and happening (in the manner of all good spies) to overhear. "What family failing?"

"You'd better ask your grandmother," Mrs. Conroy laughed, and handed the receiver to Phoebe.

"The family failing," Big Grandma told Phoebe, "is falling in love. Impractically. Desperately. Unsuitably. And usually quite hopelessly," and she sighed.

"Oh," said Phoebe thoughtfully.

"It skipped a generation with your mother. Is she listening?"

"Yes."

"She was very fortunate. It usually begins at a very young age and is often incurable."

"What utter rubbish!" exclaimed Mrs. Conroy at this point. "Take no notice, Phoebe!"

Phoebe, however, did not take no notice. On the contrary, she thought it important enough information to deserve an official communication and she wrote a note that neatly summed up her latest intelligence.

THE FAMILY FAILING
They fall in love.
Not a good thing.

She posted it behind the bedroom radiator, her most secret dead-letter box of all.

Naomi had discovered that her English literature homework was impossible. Ever since she and her sisters had been able to walk, they had taken four books each out of the library at least once a week. How many did that come to in a lifetime? And that was just library books, and did not include the books borrowed from friends, or belonging to home, or the huge number of paperbacks gulped down in furtive chunks during visits to W. H. Smith's bookstore.

Instead of trying to list everything she had read, Naomi scribbled a brief list of all that she could honestly say that she hadn't. Most of Shakespeare, she wrote, and all science fiction.

"Ruth," she said, joggling Ruth, who was droning glassy-eyed to some hideous music on her Walkman. "Who do I remind you of?"

"Who do you what?"

"Remind you of?"

"Big Grandma," said Ruth after a moment's thought.

"*Big Grandma!*" exclaimed Naomi in disgust. "I'm not a bit like Big Grandma! I meant, who would I remind you of if I reminded you of anyone in a book."

"No one," said Ruth, becoming interested in the question. "Rachel does. She reminds me of the mad woman in the attic, and Phoebe is a bit like some sort of villain. Sinister. Cruella de Ville. Or Fagin. But I can't think of anyone for you. Why?"

"I just wondered," said Naomi, who had puzzled for hours as to which heroine of literature she might possibly resemble. Perhaps she should screw up the courage in the next English literature lesson to ask straight out: "Mr. Blyton-Jones?" (For that was the unfortunate young man's name.) "Who do I remind you of?"

She felt she had almost earned the right to know. Every day she became more and more indispensable to him. No one else in the class ever had the remotest idea of which books they had heard before, or where they had got up to last time, or even what had been set for homework. Their knowledge of literature had only increased by the fact that ink on dull pages could be transformed into astonishing noise. Mr. Blyton-Jones seemed to think this such a great step forward that it didn't really matter what they heard, so long as it was loud enough. It was Naomi who worried about his reputation and gently reminded him that they had done some book or other the previous week.

"They would never have noticed," said Mr. Blyton-Jones peevishly. "Dull blear-eyed scribbling fools, and that's not slander, it's a quotation."

"Rupert Brooke," said Naomi. It was amazing how frequently she knew the source of the Temporary English teacher's quotations. More often than he did in fact.

"Do you do nothing but read books?" he asked her one day.

"Not much," said Naomi, "and write poetry, of course."

"Of course. What sort of poetry?"

"Housman," said Naomi.

"Bit beyond me, Housman," admitted Mr. Blyton-Jones in a unique moment of honesty.

"I'm sure it isn't really," said Naomi.

He did not say anything more to her in that class, and later in the day when she stopped him in the corridor to lend him her copy of Housman (with explanatory footnotes added in her best handwriting), he did not seem particularly grateful. He flicked through it, pausing to stare at the odd blank pages where Naomi had added Housman poems of her own, carefully signed so that they wouldn't confuse him.

"What did you say your name was?" he asked. "Not Andrew Marvell. Something else."

"Naomi. Naomi Conroy."

"Conroy, Conroy, Conroy," he said. "And you've got a sister at this school, haven't you?"

"Yes," admitted Naomi, and a little feeling of coldness shivered down her spine.

"They were absolutely delighted," Big Grandma told Mrs. Conroy. "I told them you would expect him any time this week . . ."

"You told them *what?*" screamed Mrs. Conroy.

"They are so pleased. He missed his English exchange visit and was very disappointed. And Julie sends her love and has invited all the girls for a week in the summer."

"Good grief! Good heavens!"

"And Monsieur Carodoc has offered us the use of his cottage any time we like. They call it a *gîte* now, of course, but nothing has really changed . . ."

"Mother!" interrupted Mrs. Conroy. "Did I hear you say that boy will be arriving here *any time this week?*"

"The sooner the better, I told them," continued Big Grandma happily. "And just think of going back to the cottage one day! We might, you know, there's nothing to stop us. They have water piped in now, as well as electricity! And a proper toilet in that little building where they used to keep hens . . ."

"I can't believe it," moaned Mrs. Conroy. "I hoped perhaps you meant he would be coming some time next year! Not next week! Go back to the beginning and tell me again!"

So Big Grandma went back to the beginning, explaining about Philippe, who was Julie's son, who was Monsieur Carodoc's daughter, who had been Big Grandma's great friend. And how nice it would be for Philippe (who was only a little older than Ruth) to visit England, and how good it would be for the girls to visit him back in France. And how conveniently it had all worked out, with the cottage in the orchard still there, and the family failing creeping (it seemed) relentlessly up on Ruth and Naomi.

"I don't know what that's got to do with having a French boy to stay," interrupted Mrs. Conroy. "And I can't imagine what makes you think it anyway. They have always had silly phases. I expect this is just another. I put it down to the hedgehog, myself."

Not to mention, continued Big Grandma, mentioning it, the need for a bit of *je ne sais quoi en famille* for poor old Rachel (and not before time, if her last school photograph was anything to go by). And since Philippe spoke perfect English and was (according to his grandfather) extraordinarily tidy, as well as being an excellent cook, he would obviously be a bargain (requiring, as he did, nothing but board and lodging and a few days' experience in an English school), even without the free French holiday thrown in by the hospitable Monsieur Carodoc.

"If you think," said Mrs. Conroy at this point, "I am going to spend any time at all in a shack in the middle of a field with a toilet in a henhouse, you have another think coming! It is not my idea of a holiday and I hope this Philippe is prepared to eat what he's given and take us as he finds us!"

"Of course he will," said Big Grandma soothingly. "I imagine he is just like his grandfather. Charming!"

"Yes, well," said Mrs. Conroy crossly. "You seem to have forgotten he has a grandmother, too, and she was not charming."

"I will overlook that remark," said Big Grandma. "You are harassed and bad-tempered because your daughters have started falling in love!"

"All this fuss about a dead hedgehog!" Mrs. Conroy exclaimed. "I am harassed and bad-tempered because you have wished an unknown French teenager on me with practically no notice!"

"He will be the least of your troubles," predicted Big Grandma cheerfully.

"I wish I could think so!"

"And if I were you, I would look beyond that dead hedgehog," Big Grandma told her, and rang off before she could reply.

Chapter Three

"AND THEN THEY ANNOUNCED Philippe would be coming. Just like that!"

"That was Big Grandma's doing."

"I suppose it was. At the time I was so dazzled at being noticed by Alan Adair that I didn't notice anything much."

"Alan Adair, among others!"

"That awful week getting ready for Philippe."

"Stop changing the subject!"

Big Grandma was right. Things had gone far beyond the dead hedgehog. Ruth, in particular, had as bad a case of the family failing as any of her ancestors had ever suffered. She no longer wondered if she was a bigamist (or possibly ambidextrous). It was as if a pathway had been found and an army was advancing. Already the numbers had doubled again. It surprised Ruth very much that the new passions, rather than replacing the old, joined forces with them instead. No sooner had Mr. Rochester and the bus driver settled down in uneasy bigamy together than they were joined by Alan Adair.

Alan Adair, wrote Ruth in her diary on Friday night. *He has started working on Saturdays in his uncle's butcher shop.*

She paused in dreamy contemplation of Alan Adair. His name alone was enough to mesmerize anyone, and Alan Adair was not just a fascinating name. He was the redheaded hero of the school, a champion tennis player and daring mountaineer. He had once ascended from the main entrance hall of the school to the second-floor library without touching the stairs, breaking his neck, or being suspended–except, of course, from his rope. The upper end of which was attached to the library door-frame. Which was wrenched away, bringing down part of the library wall. Thus cracking the ceiling of the room underneath. Which fell down the next day. And yet Alan Adair was not expelled. It was rumored in the classrooms that the principal could not have borne to part with him. He was due to enter art college in September and she excused many things on account of his artistic temperament and undoubted gift of gab.

It is the lambs' liver risotto in cooking next week, wrote Ruth. *So I will see him tomorrow.*

It was the cooking teacher's practice to make her victims responsible for collecting together their own ingredients. It was part of their homework, she explained to their parents. The parents, who were tired of being expected to conjure up obscure ingredients at a moment's notice, were only too happy to agree, but the cooks accepted their fate with very bad grace. Ruth had been as unwilling as the rest until the astonishing moment when Alan Adair (red to his wrists with gore from the mince tray) had grinned in her direction and remembered her name.

Lambs' liver risotto, wrote Ruth. *How revolting, and now I don't even get Saturdays off meeting someone I am in love with. It is wearing me out. And the bus driver has started telling me about dead hedgehogs he has passed. He does it to be kind because he thinks I am a punk rocker, although no one is these days, but I never know what to say. Egg Yolk Wendy asked the bus driver what it said on his arm. WHAT? said the driver. I said what does it say on your arm, said Wendy, because it doesn't look very nice to me. It doesn't matter to you what it says, said the driver. I suppose if you don't want to say it, then it isn't very nice, said Wendy. HELL, shouted the driver, and he started the bus really hard. You ought not to swear in front of us, said Wendy. There are some young children on this bus. I cannot get the smell of dead hedgehog out of my cooking basket. I have sprayed it with Wendy's body perfume but it is still there underneath. I have got to take Rachel to the butcher's with me tomorrow. Mum says she can come and ask about sow belly to take her mind off being May Queen.*

On Saturday morning Mrs. Conroy hurried her daughters out of the house as early as possible because the terrible problem of the inconvenient (although possibly charming) Philippe must be tackled that day. It was one thing to say in the heat of the moment that he would have to eat what he was given (of course, he would, but with what inward comments?) and take them as he found them (appalling thought), but it was quite another to put these brave words into practice. And where, in a three-bedroomed house already filled to bursting with six people, could he possibly sleep? There was only one feasible place, and that was Rachel and Phoebe's room. A camp bed would have to be brought in and their bunk beds moved in next door with Ruth and Naomi, whose single beds (which luckily were also bunks) would need to be reassembled one above the other to make room. Then, thought Mrs. Conroy, it would only be a matter of shoveling the incredible quantity of junk belonging to Rachel and Phoebe into black trash bags, repainting the walls, washing the curtains, shampooing the carpet, learning French cooking, and breaking the news to her daughters, and the family would be prepared.

"The first thing is to move the beds," she told Mr. Conroy, "and we had better get it over while the girls are out or else there will be questions and arguments forever and nothing will get done."

Ruth and Rachel's visit to the butcher's was in some ways rather a success. Alan Adair, bored almost to madness by his solitary confinement beside the chopping block, welcomed them with a torrent of conversation.

"It's so nice to see a human face," he told Ruth, "sorry, faces, I should say. Of course, your sister's is human, too. This morning has been nothing but sausages and chops and hairy old ladies asking me if I know what I'm doing. They always seem to want my uncle . . . You don't want my uncle, do you?"

"No," said Ruth, gazing adoringly at him.

"Because he's round the back, jointing a pig. Frightful business, but he enjoys it. Strange man. Have you met my aunt? His wife. A giantess. Effects of a totally carnivorous diet, you see, never stopped growing. Perfectly true. The family keeps it very quiet. Do you notice anything about the mince?"

"Not really."

"Good. Family secret, what goes into that mince. Don't buy it."

"What . . . ?" began Ruth.

"Who, you should say," Alan told her darkly. "Was it just the liver, then? Miserable stuff, the way it drips. Nothing else? Oh, don't go! Don't go and leave me in this charnel house alone!"

"There was sow belly," said Rachel eagerly, speaking for the first time. "And fat salt pork. Do you have any? Just to look at; not to buy. And do you sell horse?"

"Horse?" repeated Alan. "No. Not officially, that is. But sow belly I can produce. Belly pork we call it in the trade, although I must admit sow belly is far more evocative . . . Have you ever eaten horse?"

"No," said Rachel. "Only zebra."

"You haven't."

"I have. In Africa. Big Grandma's treat on the last day."

"How fascinating! What did it taste like?"

"Zebra," said Rachel.

"Stripy?"

"Of course not."

"Would you like a little piece of belly pork to take home for yourself?"

"Oh, yes, please," said Rachel. "Did you know I'm in our school's May Queen elections?"

"I'm not surprised," said Alan gallantly. "Oh, Ruth, don't go! You've only just come. Look at these sausages I made this morning. No. Look properly!"

"Good grief," said Ruth. "They've got buttons in."

"Yes," said Alan. "And scraps of my old school tie. Not for sale, of course, just for pleasure. Don't laugh, here comes my uncle! Hold your sow belly nicely, Rachel, and don't try to thank me! Don't say a word! Must you go? It has been so nice!"

Nice! thought Ruth as they walked home together. *Nice!* This awful helplessness. This turmoil of emotions. And for how much longer would she be able to hide her feelings from the world? What if she talked in her sleep and Naomi heard? Her dreams were full of Mr. Rochester; every night she abandoned her reputation and ran away with him to wicked foreign lands. And Mr. Rochester was the least of her troubles. It was so easy to imagine herself blurting out to, say, the bus driver, "I have fallen in love with you." Or (even worse) to Alan Adair. Or (more frightfully still) to . . .

"I shouldn't mind marrying a butcher," remarked Rachel happily, cuddling her little bundle of sow belly.

"The point is," said Ruth sternly, "would a butcher mind marrying you? What's that all down the front of your jacket?"

"Only juice," said Rachel, unwrapping her parcel to

admire its contents again and bumping as she did so into a lamppost, where somebody had inconsiderately parked their used pink bubble gum.

"Look at you!" said Ruth in disgust. "It's all in your hair! And *mind* where you're walking! Oh, Rachel! Hop to that grass and wipe your shoe! And hurry up; somebody might see me with you. Oh, no!"

A familiar figure was approaching. Ruth's heart lurched and began to pound. Rachel had only time to repeat, "Oh, no, what?" when an amazing thing happened. She was siezed and hurled over a garden fence. By Ruth.

Rachel sat in a heap on the remains of somebody's tulips and blubbered. After a while a cross old woman came out of the house and made unkind remarks, and then she was shown out by the garden gate and told never to return. Then she remembered her sow belly and went back to collect it. And then she was chased out into the street where, by great good fortune, she met Naomi and Phoebe on their way back from the library.

"It isn't fair," said Naomi. "You're supposed to be with Ruth. I don't see why I should have to have both of you."

"Ruth is a pig," said Rachel. "She picked me up and threw me into a horrible old lady's front garden."

Neither Naomi nor Phoebe appeared to think there was anything remarkable about this behavior. Naomi merely grunted, and Phoebe, who was trying to read a large-print edition of John le Carré, said nothing at all.

"And then she ran off," continued Rachel.

"Well," said Naomi reasonably, "I expect she got tired

of being seen with you. You do look a mess. Even more than usual." And she surveyed her sister's bubble-gum-tangled, sow-belly-smeared appearance with disgust.

"*And* you look like you've been sitting in mud," she added.

"I have," said Rachel.

"Well, then," said Naomi.

"I think you're horrible," said Rachel. "And Ruth. Just because that beastly man was coming."

"What man?"

"He teaches at your school. He always smirks. He's got too long legs and curly yellow hair."

"And a curly mustache?" asked Naomi.

"Yes, and a jacket that flaps."

"That's Mr. Blyton-Jones," groaned Naomi. "Oh, no! Did Mr. Blyton-Jones see you?"

"No, because beastly Ruth threw me over the fence."

"Ruth threw you over somebody's fence because Mr. Blyton-Jones was coming?"

"Is he really called that?"

"Yes," said Naomi absently, wondering why Ruth should suddenly do such a thing. Was it just natural impulse, the sort of action any reasonable person might take? Surely not. After all, Rachel did not look so very much worse than usual and, besides, if everyone who did not like her appearance took to tossing her over garden walls, she would be almost continually airborne.

But, admitted Naomi to herself, *I might do it. If Mr. Blyton-Jones was coming down the road and might see me with her, I probably would. Only it is different for me.*

"Did Ruth *explain* why she threw you over the wall?" she asked Rachel.

"I'm not speaking to any of you," said Rachel. "You think it's funny. I know you do. And Phoebe doesn't care."

"What is there to care about?" asked Phoebe. "Look! There's Ruth in front of us; you can ask her yourself. But I expect it was just the family failing coming out."

Naomi did not bother to ask Phoebe to explain this remark. Instead she hurried down the road to catch up with Ruth, who had been dawdling home by a different way. They arrived together at their garden gate and immediately forgot family failings, Temporary English teachers, and the horrors of being in love. Mrs. Conroy, who had been unable to resist having a general clear out, was carrying bulging black trash bags over to the garden wall where Mrs. Collingwood was smiling a conspiratorial smile.

". . . so much easier to get done while they are not here," they heard their mother say, "and if the bags are out of sight . . ."

"Mum!" they exclaimed in reproach, knowing too well what those bags contained. It was not the first time their possessions had been disposed of in this way.

"Not my pictures and projects!" wailed Rachel, running up from behind and grabbing the largest of the bags. "Oh, it *is* my pictures and projects! And my lovely broken doll's house . . ."

"It's nothing but rubbish that you haven't looked at for years," said her mother crossly. "What you want it for, I can't imagine. That doll's house is smashed to pieces!"

"Only because Mr. Collingwood ran over it!"

"He was terribly sorry," said Mrs. Collingwood apologetically.

"He *paid* you for it," said Mrs. Conroy sternly. "And you should never have set it up in his drive!"

"I've still got all the pieces; it only needs gluing."

"There is simply nothing that will stick that sort of plastic."

"Somebody might invent something," said Rachel, "and those pictures and projects are valuable! When I am world famous, they are just the sort of things people will want to buy."

"I don't think you are going to be world famous. Ruth! Don't tip those awful old bones out all over the garden!"

"Some of these bones are *African* bones," replied Ruth, beginning to gather them up. "I had an awful job getting them home. They're definitely not being thrown away."

"Even if I'm not world famous," said Rachel, piling her rubbish back in her trash bag and beginning to drag it back to the house, "I *might* easily be May Queen. You said yourself the chances were quite good and if Naomi is being allowed to keep those books, then . . ."

"Naomi isn't going to keep those books," said Mrs. Conroy even more crossly. "She's never made any attempt to read them. Put them back, Naomi, for goodness' sake!"

"These books," said Naomi, "are for when I have my own library. And I'm going to read them one day."

"I wish I'd never let you go to the junk sale. Ancient old copies of Dickens!"

"They might even be first editions. I wish I knew how to tell."

"Whether they are or not, they smell dreadful. They've belonged to someone who smoked and they're mildewy as well. They must have been stored somewhere damp for years and years! And *where* did you get those terrible old clothes from, Phoebe?"

"They were Emma's . . ."

"Oh," said Mrs. Conroy, suddenly much more gentle. "I'm sorry, Phoebe. I know Emma was your friend. But you've got other things of hers to remember her by that are much nicer. That lovely locket and the box of pictures . . ."

"I need them for my disguises."

"Disguises?"

"For when I'm a spy."

"Really!" exclaimed Mrs. Conroy, losing patience and grabbing Phoebe's bag. "Trash! Thank you, Mrs. Collingwood, I've tied it up. And I'll have that, too, Rachel! Stop that silly noise! And those disgusting books, Naomi! Mind your head, Mrs. Collingwood, these are heavy. Ruth, your African bones are still in the shed where you left them when you came back. These are just bits of dead sheep you picked up off the moor. There! As if I hadn't enough to worry about with this dreadful boy arriving any day."

"Dreadful boy!"

"This creature your grandmother's wished upon us. I don't know why I ever agreed."

"A boy's coming here?"

"Yes, a boy's coming here. This week. And I don't suppose for a minute he's dreadful, really, but even so . . . Philippe. I used to know his mother. French."

"French?"

"But I understand he speaks English, thank goodness! I must get the curtains down in his room!"

"His room?"

"Rachel and Phoebe's. And wash the paintwork. Your father's up there now, emulsifying the walls. Orange."

"*Orange!*"

"Pale apricot, it says on the can, but it's come out much brighter than I thought. Unless it dries paler. I didn't think pink again . . . It showed every mark . . ."

"But *why?*"

"I admit it's not ideal, but he's got to sleep somewhere. Anyway, it's only for a week or so."

"A week!"

"I expect we shall all survive. He'll be going into school with you and Naomi, Ruth. He's more or less your age . . ."

"He can't!"

"He can. I've checked with the head and she was very welcoming. Really, it's almost worth having him to get rid of that rubbish . . . those dreadful old books and Emma's ancient clothes . . ."

After her sisters had fallen asleep that night, Ruth lay awake and thought. For a while out there in the garden she had forgotten about being in love. It had been good fun in a way, the shock of hearing of the imminent arrival of an unknown French boy, the enormous discarding of rubbish, always a cheering process once one's mind had been made up to it. In the house there had been the new sleeping arrangements to inspect and moan over. Mrs. Conroy had created an overcrowded dormitory effect that nobody admired, and had insisted on it being put into use that very night.

"There won't be enough oxygen," protested Naomi.

"Well, if there isn't, there isn't," replied Mrs. Conroy heartlessly. "It will have to do."

Naomi had droned herself to sleep with dirges from Housman.

> *"Into my heart an air that kills*
> *From yon far country blows:*
> *What are those blue remembered hills,*
> *What spires, what farms are those?*
> *That is the land of lost content . . .*

"Of course you don't know what it means, Rachel! It's no good moaning at me! I didn't throw you over anyone's fence.

> *"That is the land of lost content,*
> *I see it shining plain,*
> *The happy highways where I went*
> *And cannot come again."*

Lucky old Rachel, thought Ruth. *Not knowing what it means. I don't see what else I could have done but throw her over that fence . . . Jane Eyre was only three years older than me, oh, Mr. Rochester! And Alan Adair, shut in the charnel house! "Into my heart an air that kills," I do wish the bus driver would stop telling me about dead hedgehogs. It is terribly depressing. And I wish I could read what it says on his arm. Wendy says he'll have gotten it out of a catalog. I suppose I used to live in the land of lost content without ever noticing . . .*

Chapter Four

"Big Grandma guessed that Philippe would be charming!"

"Well, so he was."

"He certainly made himself at home, right from the start."

"He specialized in letting cats out of bags!"

"We were all a bit in love with Philippe. Admit it!"

"Oh, yes, I admit it. But nothing compared . . ."

"Philippe," said Rachel that first afternoon, "will you marry me?"

"Let the poor boy get his coat off at least," said Mr. Conroy.

Philippe, who had just stepped through the door, stooped down to look at Rachel properly.

"But certainly," he said, straightening up. "How very kind! I should be charmed!"

"Rachel," said Naomi at teatime, "what about all the others you've said you're going to marry?"

"*Tous les autres?*" asked Philippe, sounding extremely shocked. "I am not the first?"

"Graham in Cumbria," said Naomi. "Martin-the-Good, who lives next door, Alan Adair from the butcher's . . ."

"And they have all agreed?" asked Philippe.

"No," said Rachel. "They just haven't said they wouldn't. And you are by far the best."

"I am so pleased to hear it."

"I shall keep them as spares."

"You won't need spares," said Philippe, twinkling at Ruth, "if you marry me!"

"Philippe," interrupted Mrs. Conroy, feeling the conversation was getting a little out of hand, "you might as well know that our Rachel can be a little bit silly at times."

"And I for one," added her husband, "shall not be holding you to any rash promises for the future, no matter how many witnesses you made them before!"

"Oh, Dad!" said Rachel.

"No shotgun marriages in this house," said Mr. Conroy.

"You will not need a shotgun," said Philippe, beaming cheerfully across at Rachel. "Mrs. Conroy, my mother sends her love. I have a letter to give you in which she tells you not to consider my feelings in any matter or discommode yourself in any way."

"Too late," said Ruth. "We are discommoded already. I'll show you our bedroom . . ."

"Fetid cell," interrupted Naomi.

"Fetid cell, then, after tea and you'll see what I mean. And the carpet in your room still isn't dry."

"Nothing could matter less."

"I have turned the heating up full," said Mrs. Conroy apologetically, "and, Philippe, if there's anything you like to eat that isn't here, you only have to say."

"Ask for smoked salmon and truffles," urged Ruth.

"This is much nicer than smoked salmon and truffles," he replied, smiling at Mrs. Conroy, and Mrs. Conroy, who had worried more about feeding Philippe than anything else she could remember since Phoebe was born, smiled lovingly back.

"He is charming," she reported to Big Grandma on the telephone that evening. "We are all completely smitten . . . No, he hasn't mentioned his grandfather . . . No, I really couldn't say what color his eyes are. Brown, I should think, or gray. Very dark . . . He is in the kitchen washing up with the girls . . . Well, he absolutely insisted . . . Yes, all getting on very well. He has promised to marry Rachel and was very kind when we discovered Phoebe going through his bags . . . No, no photographs. A telescope, Phoebe thought, but it turned out to be a bottle of cognac. Quite legal, not smuggled . . ."

Philippe's eyes were black and he fitted into the Conroy house as if he had known them forever.

"He is a paragon," said Ruth, watching as he scraped and stacked the supper plates.

"He will need to be," replied Naomi, "if he is going to marry Rachel."

"I still can't work out exactly why he's come," said Phoebe.

"To improve my English," Philippe told her seriously. "We have examinations very soon. I beg that none of you will speak to me in French."

"We won't," said Naomi.

"We can't," said Rachel.

"What's so important about learning English?" asked Phoebe suspiciously, her mind still on espionage.

"Americans speak it," said Philippe, and burst out laughing at their insulted faces. "But of course there are other reasons for learning English. Now these plates are organized. Who will wash?"

Ruth washed. Naomi dried. Phoebe polished the glasses and knives (a refinement no Conroy had ever considered necessary before), and Rachel put away. Philippe emptied the trash, watered the potted plants, wiped the surfaces, swept the floor, discussed English literature with Naomi, completed in seconds Ruth's French homework, and promised to help Rachel prepare for the May Queen elections that were to take place the next day.

"I didn't think French people liked queens," remarked Phoebe. "Look at that one whose head you cut off for knitting and eating cake."

"I would never cut off a head for eating cake," Philippe assured her. "Knitting perhaps, yes. But is it not rather late in the month for choosing a May Queen?"

"We can only have the Thin One's dad's milk-float for a chariot every other Monday," explained Rachel. "Because that's his half day. It's being decorated with pink paper roses and leaves and butterflies and plastic grass and a throne. Shall I show you the list?"

"The list?"

"The May Queen list with my name on it."

"Oh, yes, please."

"I'll fetch it!"

"Philippe," Ruth said when Rachel had scurried away. "Mum says we shouldn't encourage her too much about being a May Queen because she'll never be chosen and it really isn't fair to raise her hopes."

"Why should she not be chosen?" asked Philippe.

"They're supposed to vote for the kindest and most helpful and hardworking as well as what they look like," explained Ruth. "And Rachel sulks a lot and she isn't even clean most of the time . . ."

"She should never have been nominated," said Naomi severely. "We're not being horrible; we're just facing facts. It's us that'll have to live with her when she's not elected."

"Perhaps something might be arranged?" suggested Philippe.

"You can't bribe a whole school; we've thought of that."

"Listen!" interrupted Phoebe. "What's that shouting?"

The shouting was Rachel announcing that the house was on fire. At first it seemed as if she might almost be right; no flames or smoke were visible, but upstairs there was a definite smell of burning in the air. Mr. Conroy hurried outside to check the chimney; Mrs. Conroy rushed to the kitchen and the central heating boiler, and while they were occupied Philippe, sniffing like a bloodhound, traced the smell to his bedroom, where the radiator, turned on to dry the carpet, was diligently cooking the contents of Phoebe's most private dead-letter box of all.

"It's stuffed full of paper behind here," announced Naomi, flattening her face against the wall to peer into the gap. "And it's scorching because Mum turned the radiator up so high to dry the carpet. Go and shout and tell them it's all right. *No, Rachel!*"

But she was too late, and before Naomi could even duck out of the way, Rachel had seized the large vase of tulips decorating the windowsill and hurled its contents at the source of the investigation. When Mrs. Conroy arrived on the scene, she found Ruth and Naomi dripping with tulip water, Rachel dripping with tears, and Philippe howling with laughter on the carpet.

"Get up, Philippe!" she said crossly. "This carpet is still damp; you will ruin that lovely sweater. You two Big Ones, for goodness' sake go and get changed, and, Rachel, it's time for your bath. Off you go and I'll come and wash your hair in a minute. Phoebe, what are you doing with that coat hanger?"

"There's paper stuck behind the radiator. That's what's scorching."

"Let me help," said Philippe.

"It's private messages to myself."

"Well," began Mrs. Conroy, "let Philippe . . . *Rachel!* You can't run about with nothing on when we have guests in the house. Oh . . ." And she disappeared and slammed the door just as Philippe, who had been industriously fishing with the coat hanger, managed to drag up a curled piece of paper. On it was inscribed in large black letters:

DEAD LETTER BOX NUMBER ONE

"Very strange," he remarked to Phoebe. "I wonder what it means."

Phoebe sighed with relief. He couldn't read it. He could speak English, but reading and writing it were obviously beyond him. It was not really surprising at all, when she thought about it. Hadn't she herself been able to speak English years and years before she had been able to read and write?

Philippe scooped again with the coat hanger and produced another piece of paper, slightly damp and rather torn but still perfectly legible:

Ruth has got the family failing very badly indeed.

"Do you know what it means?" she asked Philippe, just to check for certain that he really could not read.

"It concerns Ruth? Something to do with Ruth?"

I was right, Phoebe told herself with satisfaction, and she wrote herself a dead-letter box note in her head:

Philippe speaks but cannot read.

Good, thought Phoebe, and then watched complacently as one by one Philippe retrieved, smoothed out, and handed over all the family secrets of the last few months.

Philippe has been here since just before teatime, wrote Ruth in her diary that night. *And I have not fallen in love with him. Thank goodness. Naomi says he is laughing at us all the time . . .*

Ruth paused and thought for a moment and then crossed out "Naomi says" and made the *h* of "he" a capital letter. No point in pretending there was any doubt about the matter.

Even Phoebe likes him. She read him a bedtime story.

"Well, he can't read," Phoebe explained. "Or write."

"I can," said Philippe indignantly. "I have been reading and writing since I was five years old."

"Only French," said Phoebe, causing Philippe to collapse with laughter once again.

"In France," Mr. Conroy explained to Phoebe, "it is the custom to teach the children their native language."

"Well, I don't see why," replied Phoebe. "English would be much more useful and then we wouldn't have to learn French."

"Anyway," Naomi interrupted, "Philippe can read. He's read loads of the same books as me."

"Only in translation," admitted Philippe. "But do not forget the story, Phoebe. What is it entitled?"

"*Tinker, Tailor, Soldier, Spy,*" said Phoebe, watching him to see if he flinched. "I don't know how you'll manage at Ruth and Naomi's school. You should come with me and Rachel. There are plenty of people in my class who can't read or write."

Ruth made a mental list of everyone she had fallen in love with, and lay on her bed contemplating it. The bus driver was the worst.

"The bus driver is the worst what?" asked Naomi, and Ruth realized with horror that she must have spoken aloud.

"Oh," she said in confusion, "worst to arrange. For Philippe. So he could come with us to school. I had to ask about it this afternoon."

"I know, but the driver didn't mind, did he?"

"He said he'd have to pay. And I said, 'Thank you,' and he said, 'No problem. Since it's you.' And I said, 'Thank you, thank you, thank you, thank you.'"

"Yes, I heard you saying that. I thought for a minute he'd given you another dead hedgehog or something. Do you like him?"

"Who?" asked Ruth. "The bus driver?"

"Philippe."

"Oh," said Ruth. "Yes, quite. Do you?"

"Quite," said Naomi cautiously.

I guessed about Ruth and the bus driver ages ago, thought Phoebe sleepily. *He was the first. I hope I don't get the family failing.*

Above her Rachel gave a tiny snuffling snore.

"Not much like a May Queen," Phoebe commented out loud.

"We thought you were asleep!"

"Well, I wasn't. Philippe's got a plan about Rachel, did you know?"

"What sort of plan?"

"To make her May Queen."

"What could he possibly do?"

"I don't know. Soap?"

"It would take more than soap," said Naomi. "It would take a miracle!"

On Friday Philippe performed the miracle. Rachel came home from school elected May Queen.

"Flew home from school," Mrs. Conroy told her husband at suppertime. "She hasn't touched ground yet."

"Philippe," said Mr. Conroy when they happened to be alone for a moment, "what did you do?"

"*Moi?*" asked Philippe innocently.

"I know you walked them to school."

"Mrs. Conroy said I might."

"Go on."

"I walked to school with Rachel and Phoebe," said Philippe meekly. "And signed a few autographs. And came home."

"A few autographs?"

"I think about two hundred or so. I did not count. Rachel kept introducing new friends."

"Did they think you were someone famous?"

"No, no," said Philippe hastily. "My English, as you are aware, is very bad, but I understand they thought I was the younger brother of some French international football player. . . ."

"Philippe!"

"So I signed my name, very untidily, and put some kisses . . ."

"And Rachel is May Queen?"

"Of course she is also very beautiful."

"Very beautiful," said Mr. Conroy. "Shake! Half my kingdom any day you ask for it!"

"Thank you," said Philippe.

Never had Mr. Conroy taken to someone so quickly. There followed a most amazing weekend.

"Philippe must not go home without a look at London," he announced on Friday night. "Early to bed and early to rise. We'll catch a train down in the morning and show Rachel Buckingham Palace. And Naomi the Houses of Parliament. And Ruth the zoo. And Phoebe . . ."

"What?" asked Phoebe.

"The Underground," said Mr. Conroy. "And on Sunday we'll drive into the country and find a proper English pub for lunch, and on Monday we'll have the May Queen's coronation! I shall take the afternoon off work."

"And when will Rachel attend the salon for her hair?" asked Philippe.

There was a flabbergasted silence.

"Philippe!" said Mrs. Conroy faintly. "Do you think Rachel ought to go to the hairdresser's?"

"*Mais oui!*" said Philippe, nodding violently. "*Certainement!*"

"But she's always had that braid!"

"I did not mean to be rude."

"No," said Mrs. Conroy. "You're probably right. I'm sure you're right. She can go on Monday morning, first thing."

"Cut off my hair?" asked Rachel.

"I will come with you," promised Philippe.

"But I want to grow it long enough to sit on."

"*Pourquoi?*" asked Philippe reasonably. "Is it not curly? You should have it cut like feathers. You will be transformed."

Ruth and Naomi were allowed out of school early on Monday afternoon so that they could catch the tail end of the May Queen procession. They arrived at the playing field just as the celebrations were coming to an end. There was the maypole, a tangle of streamers, the Morris men (who had refused to dance unless allowed to wear football shirts and no bells); there was the milk-float, a bower of plastic grass and roses, and there was the throne.

"Oh!" exclaimed Ruth in dismay. "I knew it must be a mistake! Poor old Rachel."

"Isn't it her?"

"Of course it isn't."

"No, you're right. Crikey! But there's Philippe taking photographs. That's a bit heartless! And I can see Mum and Dad with Phoebe . . . Ruth!"

"What?"

"It *is* Rachel!"

"Where?"

"On the throne. Look!"

"It can't be!"

"Transformed!"

"Good grief!"

"Philippe said she would be transformed."

Finally Philippe and Mrs. Conroy ran out of film. The maypole was dismantled, the milk-float was stripped of its flowers, the school caretaker arrived to lock the gates, Mr. Conroy renewed his offer to Philippe of half his kingdom and escorted his family home. Supper was eaten, toasts were drunk, darkness fell.

Late in the night Rachel rustled and bumped in the top bunk. In the bed beneath Phoebe sighed. No use protesting; Rachel was beyond reason. It had been a terrible job getting her down from the throne. She had had to be lured away with continental chocolates.

"Stop thumping about!" hissed Naomi through the dark.

"I can't get to sleep. My head hurts."

"Well, take it off, then."

"Take my head off?"

"Take the crown off!"

"No," said Rachel.

Chapter Five

"IT WAS AFTER PHILIPPE WENT HOME that you cracked!"

"I didn't crack. I just had a very severe case of the family failing and it was too much for me. Anyway, you were not exactly sensible yourself. I haven't forgotten your hair!"

"My hair was Philippe's fault. Poor Mum lost patience and telephoned Big Grandma to take us away."

"Which she did."

"Not very gracefully! It was partly kindness and partly . . ."

"Cover."

On Tuesday Philippe went to school for the first time with Ruth and Naomi. He spoke such perfect English, was so extremely thin, so extraordinarily French, and so utterly charming that he was an immediate success. He wandered between Ruth's and Naomi's classes, enchanting everyone he met, noticing everything, constantly amused by the antics of the English. He seemed to be everywhere; neither Ruth nor Naomi could ever be sure just when he would appear, or who would be the next victim of his glamour.

Hearts were handed over by the dozen. It was rather like being responsible for a half-tame unicorn, slightly alarming but with a lot of reflected glory. Alan Adair went out of his way to welcome him to the school. Egg Yolk Wendy (whose life was dedicated to Women's Lib and hairdressing) melted completely after one glance from his gleaming black eyes.

"Whose is he?" she asked Ruth. "Yours or Naomi's?"

"He's going to marry Rachel," Ruth told her.

Wendy laughed.

"You may laugh," said Ruth. "But he hasn't said he wouldn't!"

The aspect of school that Philippe appeared to enjoy the most was Mr. Blyton-Jones's English lessons. He took them in double doses every day, once with Naomi's class, and later on with Ruth's.

"To get out of math," said Ruth.

"To improve my English," said Philippe, and refused to take any notice when Ruth pointed out that his English was already far better than that of Mr. Blyton-Jones. Philippe enjoyed English literature. The first lesson he witnessed caused him to almost suffocate with painful laughter. That morning Mr. Blyton-Jones had produced *The Mill on the Floss* from his pocket, and begun at the end with the death by drowning of the hero and heroine. Philippe's laughter grew into agony as the lesson progressed and Mr. Blyton-Jones (always concentrating on the most harrowing passages) skipped his way backward to the start of the book before concluding with a Shakespearean sonnet, a couple of extremely bloodthirsty pages from *The*

Machine Gunners, and several smoldering comments on the misplaced sense of humor of foreigners.

"Excuse me, I beg," pleaded Philippe with the irate Temporary English teacher when the lesson was over and the rest of the class had gone. "It was not you. It was their faces."

"What?"

"Their faces as you read."

"I cannot be responsible for their faces," said Mr. Blyton-Jones peevishly.

"I shall not laugh again," promised Philippe, and kept his word. He was nothing if not diplomatic.

"I don't know how we shall manage without him," remarked Mrs. Conroy as the days passed by. Never had there been so few quarrels in the house, or had rooms remained so tidy, or homework been accomplished so painlessly, and it was all due to Philippe and his seemingly endless supply of tact and good humor.

"Ironing I adore," he told the besotted Mrs. Conroy, "also to clean the bath, and if Phoebe so kindly reads to me every night why may I not polish her shoes?"

Mrs. Conroy drew the line at polishing Phoebe's shoes, but she did permit Philippe to cook, and he produced the first cheese soufflé ever to appear at the Conroy table.

"I'm glad you're marrying me," said Rachel.

After his first experience with English literature Philippe sat through everything Mr. Blyton-Jones chose to hurl at his victims looking like someone half-asleep in an empty room. His expression was invariably an unearthly blank. No detail escaped him, however. On his last afternoon, while he helped Mrs. Conroy and Ruth prepare his good-bye supper, he attempted to cheer them up with an account of the lesson, and his description was far from blank.

"This terrible noise of words," he explained, "and all the students so confused. Except for Ruth and Naomi, of course; they are not confused . . . Shall I make salad dressing or mayonnaise?"

"*Can* you make mayonnaise?"

"*Mais oui.* I always make the mayonnaise for my mother. No, Ruth and Naomi are not confused, but even worse: They are in love!"

"Don't be ridiculous, Philippe!" said Mrs. Conroy, laughing.

"*Mais c'est vrai,* is it not, Ruth?"

"No!" snapped Ruth.

"At his approach one day did you not once throw poor Rachel over a garden wall?"

"Ruth!" exclaimed Mrs. Conroy.

"It was ages ago and she looked such a scruff. Anyone would have done it. Naomi said so, too."

"But Naomi is also in love with the same Mr. Blyton-Jones," pointed out Philippe. "He cannot tell them apart!"

"What rubbish!" said Mrs. Conroy cheerfully. "They are not at all alike."

"Who aren't?" demanded Naomi, coming in at that moment. "What's that awful wobbly-looking muck, Philippe?"

"Mayonnaise," said Philippe, looking hurt. "I was telling Mrs. Conroy how your Mr. Blyton-Jones confuses Ruth and you in his mind."

This was exactly the suspicion that had recently begun to form in Naomi's mind and she was not pleased to hear it spoken aloud.

"Is this your good-bye supper, then?" she remarked.

"Yes, and I wish I did not have to leave so soon. You have all been so amusing."

"It doesn't feel soon to me," said Naomi. "And I must say it'll be nice to have a change from all this disgusting French cooking."

"Yes," agreed Ruth, who was also furious. "Snail omelette, snail omelette, snail omelette, day after day."

"Take no notice, Philippe!" said Mrs. Conroy, laughing, but Philippe happened to be sensitive about his cooking, and had heard more than one unkind reference to snails during his stay in England; for once, his temper got the better of him.

"Both of you sisters, and both of you adoring him! Why should he not mistake your names?" he asked as Naomi banged through the fridge in search of tomato ketchup. "One omelette have I cooked and no snails! But no matter, anyway, if he finds you alike," he added, raising his voice as Naomi stamped out of the room. "Both can admire. And Ruth still has her bus driver and Alan Adair . . . *Oh!*"

"*Ruth!*" exclaimed Mrs. Conroy. "Philippe! That lovely mayonnaise! Put your head under the faucet, Philippe! *Ruth, apologize at once!*"

"No, no," protested Philippe, wiping mayonnaise from his eyes. "It is I who should apologize. I am so sorry, Ruth. It was the snails that made me so angry . . ."

But Ruth had gone. It was not so much what Philippe had said that was so devastating, but the fact that he had guessed at all. And if she had not been so handy with the mayonnaise, who else might he have added to his list? "*Et moi!*" she could imagine him finishing triumphantly. Could he have possibly noticed that she had not remained unaffected by his charms? It seemed only too likely. Lucky, lucky Rachel, to have been born so shameless!

I am fed up with being in love, she wrote grimly in her diary that night.

The next day was Thursday. Philippe left early in the morning to catch a train to London, where a friend of his family was to meet him and travel with him to France. He had been with the Conroys for two weeks and without him it was as if all the colors of the world had suddenly faded to black and white.

"It seems ages and ages since I was May Queen," remarked Rachel as she trudged to school with Phoebe.

"You've still got your crown," said Phoebe. "And your hair."

Rachel's hair was still being regarded as a small miracle. She really had been transformed. People who had known her all her life now barely recognized her.

"It's like a disguise," said Phoebe.

"What is?"

"Your hair."

"Philippe says it's how it should have been all the time. I hope he doesn't forget he promised to marry me."

"What you should worry about is who else he promises to marry."

"Did he you?" Rachel asked in alarm.

"No."

"Well, he won't have done Ruth and Naomi. They are hardly speaking to him."

"Did you know Ruth tipped mayonnaise all over his head last night?"

"Mayonnaise?"

"I saw him in the bathroom washing it off."

"What a waste!"

"So that's definitely Ruth ruled out, then!"

"So it is," said Rachel, cheering up a little.

Ruth had never felt so ruled out in her life. She felt hopeless. Extinguished. The family failing had finally been too much for her. All at once she could not face another day of bus drivers, Temporary English teachers, redheaded classmates, and the horrible possibility of adding to the list.

Mrs. Conroy had been astonishingly understanding and sent Naomi to school alone.

"There's only today and tomorrow and then it's half-term," she said to Ruth. "And you look tired out. I do hope you're not going to be ill."

"This is much worse than being ill," Ruth replied miserably. "At least when you're ill you get better again."

"I did hope you wouldn't start being silly about boys," said Mrs. Conroy, sighing. "Oh, well, perhaps you just need a holiday. At least Naomi is being sensible."

This was speaking too soon. Naomi arrived home that afternoon very late, very sulky, and very defiant, and from the moment she stepped through the door it was perfectly obvious that she had been far from sensible.

"Naomi!" exclaimed Mrs. Conroy. "Whatever, *whatever* have you done?"

"I knew you'd be like that," said Naomi. "Blaming me!"

"Well, who are we supposed to blame?"

Naomi said if they wanted to blame anyone they should blame Philippe. She had only changed her image, like Rachel had done . . .

"Like me?" said Rachel indignantly.

. . . And it was no good them asking and asking about who had done it, because she had promised not to say. And of course it wouldn't wash out: What was the good of changing one's image if it was going to change back again a few days later? And at least no one could mistake her for Ruth anymore. And she didn't know what all the fuss was about; after all, it was her head, wasn't it? At this point, Naomi burst into most uncharacteristic tears, but they gathered (between sobs) that if anyone was to be held accountable, it should be Big Grandma, who had wished Philippe with his revelations and transformations upon them in the first place. And then her complaints grew more general, taking in the whole of the thirteen and a half years of injustice that she had suffered at the hands of her callous and undeserving family, and by now everyone had stopped listening because they had heard it all before.

"Actually," said Rachel, some time later in the evening, "I quite like it." And this, to Naomi, was the worst blow of all.

"Who did it?" asked Ruth when they were in bed that night.

"What does it matter who did it?" asked Naomi, with

Rachel's words still rankling in her heart.

"Did you mean it to be blue?"

"Of course I didn't."

"What, then?"

"Purple. It said purple on the kit we bought."

"Wasn't it done at a proper hairdresser's, then?"

"Of course it wasn't done at a proper hairdresser's! Does it look like it was done at a proper hairdresser's?" snapped Naomi. "It was Egg Yolk Wendy that did it and don't you ever dare tell anyone because I promised I wouldn't. She's very upset. She says it could ruin her career."

"Serve her right."

"What does it matter?" said Naomi wearily. "My hair's not the worst thing."

"What is, then?"

"Oh, well," said Naomi. "You might as well know. The worst thing was Mr. Blyton-Jones."

"What's Mr. Blyton-Jones got to do with it?"

"You know Egg Yolk Wendy's sister?"

"Not Fat-Slob-and-One-Leg?"

"Yes, Fat-Slob-and-One-Leg."

"Oh, no!"

Fat-Slob-and-One-Leg was Wendy's big sister.

"Very big sister," Ruth had once remarked.

"She does bust exercises," Wendy told her treacherously.

"To make it smaller?"

"No, stupid!"

Wendy's big sister wore such tight skirts that sitting down in public was impossible. Instead she lolled against walls, usually standing on one leg.

"To give the other one a rest," suggested Naomi.

Her name was Dawn and she did not have a kind heart.

"You moan about your sisters," Wendy said to Ruth and Naomi, "but at least they don't wear nose-rings!" Wendy did not encourage her friends to call her sister Dawn. "Fat-Slob-and-One-Leg suits her much better."

"It's a bit of a mouthful."

"Well, you thought of it."

"Me and Wendy were in her bedroom staring at my hair in the mirror," Naomi told Ruth, "when we heard talking in the hall. Wendy's big sister and Mr. Blyton-Jones. Fat-Slob-and-One-Leg knew we were there, but she must have thought we'd gone. We weren't making any noise, you know, just staring."

"Are you alone?" Naomi and Wendy heard Mr. Blyton-Jones inquire. "Alone and paley loitering?"

("Keats," explained Naomi to Ruth.

"I know," said Ruth.)

"Definitely loitering," Fat-Slob-and-One-Leg had replied, and then Naomi and Wendy had sat in disgusted silence while a squelchy sort of mumbling went on below.

"I didn't know she knew him," hissed Naomi to Wendy.

"Neither did I."

"Actually, I'm supposed to be staying at home with my sister," Fat-Slob-and-One-Leg remarked when the squelching broke off.

"I didn't know you had a sister," said Mr. Blyton-Jones in an interested voice. "Older?"

"Much younger. You teach her. Her and her friend are

supposed to be here but they seem to have disappeared. You must know them."

"Must I?"

"They adore you."

"Well, they all do."

"Wendy, she's called, and her friend is Ruth. Or Naomi. I can never remember which."

"Neither can I," said Mr. Blyton-Jones, and laughed.

"Heartless!" said Fat-Slob-and-One-Leg.

"One teenage mutant school-uniform wearer looks much like another to me," Mr. Blyton-Jones said airily. "Couldn't possibly remember them all. My job is merely to spill the pearls of English literature on their uncomprehending ears!"

("Uncomprehending?" interrupted Ruth. "Is that what he said?"

"Yes."

"Every lesson I have to help him out!"

"So do I.")

"I ask myself," Mr. Blyton-Jones continued, his voice rising with pleasure, because this was a favorite subject, "is this what I went to university for?"

"Are we going out?" asked Fat-Slob-and-One-Leg, sounding extremely bored. "Or not?"

"One of those girls you've had here, can never remember which . . ."

"He's talking about you and Ruth," whispered Wendy to Naomi.

". . . writes poetry!" Mr. Blyton-Jones snorted with laughter. "Housman! Hysterical!"

"Must be," said Fat-Slob-and-One-Leg irritably. "I always used to try to escape English myself."

"Me, too," said Mr. Blyton-Jones.

("Did he really say that?" asked Ruth.

"Yes."

"Then what?"

"Then it was all quiet for ages and it was getting really late and we couldn't think of anything to do about my hair and, anyway, I didn't really care anymore . . .")

"Do you think they've gone?" Naomi asked Wendy.

"They're probably in the sitting room."

"I'm going, then."

"I'm really sorry."

"It's not your fault."

"I suppose you *did* choose the dye," said Wendy, extremely surprised at this magnanimity, "but I cut it!"

"Oh, my hair!" exclaimed Naomi, who had forgotten her hair and assumed Wendy was apologizing for her sister's behavior with the appalling Mr. Blyton-Jones. "Yes, my hair's your fault. *Don't* start crying again! I said I wouldn't tell Mum and Dad. I'm going to make a dash for it before they come out."

They leaned over the bannister and the house seemed silent. The hall was empty and the living room door shut.

("Shut?" asked Ruth.

"Yes, but that wasn't where they were. They were on the porch. I ran straight into them.")

"Oi!" shouted Fat-Slob-and-One-Leg as she was knocked from the Temporary English teacher's embrace. "Mind my tights!"

Naomi, who had replaced Fat-Slob-and-One-Leg's position in the arms of Mr. Blyton-Jones, struggled to break free.

"Who is it?" demanded her captor, holding on tight. "Your sister?"

"No, no, no," said Fat-Slob-and-One-Leg, giggling hysterically. "Her hair's yellow. It must be that friend I told you about."

"I'm sure I don't teach anyone with blue hair. I'd have noticed. Do I teach you?"

"No," said Naomi through gritted teeth.

"Thank goodness for that," said Mr. Blyton-Jones, and let go.

"And you needn't sniff like that," Naomi told Ruth. "He doesn't teach me. He's never taught me a single thing! I have to teach him! And he didn't even know who I was! He was just glad that no one who knew him had caught him with Fat-Slob-and-One-Leg. And the things he said!"

"Teenage mutant school-uniform wearers!" said Ruth.

"And he called my poetry hysterical."

"And he said he used to try to escape English."

"And said we all adore him."

"And said he couldn't tell us apart."

"I always guessed he couldn't tell us apart," said Naomi sadly.

"That's not really why you dyed your hair, is it?"

"Oh, shut up!"

"Is it?"

"Of course not!"

"Naomi!"

"Shut up! Shut up! Shut up!" said Naomi. "I'm going to sleep."

Ruth did not go to sleep. She lay awake and counted them up: bus driver and Mr. Rochester. Alan Adair. Philippe. Mr. Blyton-Jones.

Not Mr. Blyton-Jones, she thought a few minutes later.

While they were asleep, Mrs. Conroy, between tiredness and crossness and the complications of having three daughters in love and the fourth a prospective international spy, decided that there was some justice in Naomi's blaming of Big Grandma for the events of the evening. She telephoned that night to tell her so.

Chapter Six

"SEASICKNESS AND LOVESICKNESS combined! Big Grandma knew what she was doing when she took us abroad to cure us of the family failing."

"That holiday in France was our first abroad. Our first real abroad, I mean."

"What about Africa?"

"France was much more abroad than Africa."

"*Moi?*" asked Big Grandma, sounding exactly like Philippe, when, after hours and hours of trying, Mrs. Conroy finally got through to her and repeated Naomi's accusation. "What exactly have you telephoned for? To tell me off?"

"There was something I wanted to ask you, but first tell me why you've suddenly gone all French."

"Catching," said Big Grandma airily. "I've been talking to Charles . . ."

"Is that why your telephone has been engaged all this time?"

"Quite possibly."

"Really, Mother! At your age!"

"What do you mean, at my age?" demanded Big Grandma. "Of course at my age! When you get to seventy you haven't a day to waste, and I have wasted years! I am just beginning to realize."

"Realize what?"

"That I am not getting any younger and neither are my friends. Anyway, I'm listening now, so tell me what you wanted to ask me. And what is it I'm supposed to have done?"

"Introduced Philippe into the household. And I was calling to ask you if you would mind having the girls to stay this half-term holiday. Ruth and Naomi at least. Ruth definitely could do with a change of scene; she has gotten all worked up about some boy at school . . ."

"The family failing! What did I tell you? I knew it must be more than a dead hedgehog!"

"Yes, well, you were right. Not that he isn't a pleasant boy, but I am afraid he is not the only one . . ."

"Poor, poor Ruth!"

"According to Philippe, that is. He seemed to understand it all. And since he let out what he had noticed, Naomi has been very cross indeed. Apparently some teacher she is fond of has been mistaking her for Ruth. And so she thought she could do with a change of appearance. Oh, dear! Of course, Philippe transformed Rachel so successfully from the neck up, so to speak, that naturally Naomi . . ."

"Is it very drastic?"

"Inch-long spikes. Gelled, she says."

"Rather exciting."

"And dyed purple."

"Purple?"

"Well, bluish purple."

"Lavender?"

"Much, much brighter."

"Goodness," said Big Grandma, and there was a long silence during which it became apparent that she was not going to say that her two eldest granddaughters must both come and visit at once. Big Grandma, it seemed, did not want Ruth and Naomi wandering about the village lovesick and with purple hair, no matter (as she explained to Mrs. Conroy) how bluish the actual shade of purple.

"And probably falling in love with the neighbors to boot," said Big Grandma. "Most embarrassing! Don't forget I have to live here!" She suggested that Mrs. Conroy redye Naomi and tell Ruth to pull herself together, and rang off rather crossly.

"So much for the extended family!" said Mrs. Conroy to herself, and was just making her mind up to endure an awful and exhausting half-term holiday when her husband called to tell her that Big Grandma was back on the telephone again.

"I have reconsidered . . ." she began, and waves and waves of thankfulness swept over Mrs. Conroy.

". . . I'm not having them in the village. That would be too much. But if you would really like them to have a change, I will take them to France . . ."

"To *France!*"

"After all, what could be more reasonable than for a grandmother to take her grandchildren on holiday? Quite innocent and respectable, I should have thought."

"But are you sure you could manage?"

"I took them to Africa, didn't I? What possible harm could they come to in Charles Carodoc's apple orchard?"

"Mother!"

"It would be absolutely perfect. A complete change of scene. And nobody will bother about Naomi's hair over there. They will just put it down to her being English; and when she gets back she can blame it on France. What could be more simple?"

"But what about getting them ready?"

"What is there to get? They have passports. They don't need inoculations. I will sort out some insurance. Washing things. Night things. A change or two of clothes and some pocket money. I will drive down tomorrow for an early Saturday start. Plenty of room, one in the front and three in the back . . ."

"You're thinking of taking Rachel and Phoebe *as well?*"

"Of course. They will be excellent cover."

"*Excellent cover?* Oh, company! Cover, I thought you said . . ."

"Company," repeated Big Grandma hastily. "Excellent company. Now don't start arguing! It takes so much time and you know I always win in the end!"

"But what does Monsieur Carodoc say to all this?"

"It was his idea," said Big Grandma triumphantly.

"And Madame Carodoc?"

"Must dash!" said Big Grandma, and rang off.

✼ ✼ ✼

"Come on!" ordered Big Grandma. "Get packing! Of course you don't want to go! You people never want to go anywhere when it comes to the crunch."

"That's true," agreed Mrs. Conroy. "The fuss you all made about going to Cumbria to visit Big Grandma that first summer! You didn't even want to go to Africa when it came to the last minute, and look what a wonderful time you had when you got there!"

The girls glanced rather sheepishly at Big Grandma at this remark, but much to their relief she made no comment. Never since the day it happened had she given any sign at all of remembering that the wonderful time in Africa had been preceded by a miserable twenty-four hours when they had all four of them lost courage and begged to be taken home. There was a definite nobleness in the way Big Grandma had wiped that incident from her memory, and her granddaughters remembered it. They did as they were told, and packed.

"Shall we go through the Channel Tunnel?" asked Phoebe hopefully.

"Heavens, no!" exclaimed Big Grandma. "I don't believe in it at all."

"How can you not believe in it?" demanded Phoebe. "You must have seen it on the news."

"Well, of course I believe it *exists*, my dear Phoebe," said Big Grandma. "I just don't believe it should have been *dug*. And I don't propose to encourage the government by using it."

"Do you think they will be saying in Whitehall, 'Oh,

no! Big Grandma's not using the Channel Tunnel?'" asked Naomi.

"'We never should have dug it; we'd better fill it in,'" added Ruth, joining in and cheering up for a moment because it was so nice to have Big Grandma taking over in her old Big Grandma-ish way.

"'Very unencouraging,'" said Naomi. "The poor prime minister. 'First the National Lottery,' he will say. 'She didn't believe in that either, and it had to go. And now this . . .'"

"Come on, Naomi!" said Mrs. Conroy, laughing. "Pack! There's four hats in this bag so far, and the complete works of that gloomy Housman and nothing else . . . Is your bag done, Rachel? Aren't you taking your crown?"

"I shall be *wearing* my crown," said Rachel.

"Not on the ferry," said Big Grandma hurriedly. "To drive down, perhaps, but after that it must go in a bag. I don't want to have to witness any tragedies at sea. Naomi, are you sure you want to keep your hair that color?"

"It's better than brown," said Naomi. "Brown just looked like a dead hedgehog."

"Yes, I suppose it must have. Oh, Ruth, don't look so miserable! I promise you'll be far too busy in France to fall in love."

If Ruth had been less engulfed in her dead hedgehog memories, she would have detected an ominous note in this promise, but as it was she simply sighed and carried her bag out to the car. She didn't know which was worse: the awfulness of living in the same country as the bus driver, and Alan Adair, or the awfulness of leaving it behind.

But at least I can take Mr. Rochester with me, she thought, hugging her battered copy of *Jane Eyre* to her chest. *And Philippe . . .*

That was the first bit of bad news. Philippe, Big Grandma told them as they drove south through England in a chilling gray dawn, lived quite some distance from where they were to stay.

"His grandfather's farm is right out in the countryside," she told them.

"Right out in the countryside?"

"Of course there is a village. A few shops and a post office just a nice walk away."

There was a long silence during which the girls reviewed their prospects of a pleasant holiday. Naomi broke it, voicing for the first time their innermost fears.

"I suppose they're all going to be speaking French."

"Who?"

"Everyone over there."

"The French," said Big Grandma, "will most probably speak French. It is what comes naturally to them."

"They can all speak English as well, though," said Rachel cheerfully. "I've seen them doing it on TV when they're being interviewed for the news. Everyone they ask can speak proper English. They just do it with funny voices, that's all."

"French accents," corrected Big Grandma, "not funny voices. And that is a common delusion, Rachel, but pause and reflect! Would anyone bother to broadcast the ones who couldn't?"

"Philippe spoke English as good as me," argued Rachel, undaunted.

"I gather Philippe is very like his grandfather," said Big Grandma dreamily. "Unusually gifted in every way . . . Hold tight, everyone, now, I'm going to put my foot down. We must make the lunchtime ferry; we are sailing by a longish route. The farther we go by sea, the less distance there will be to drive on the other side. Do look out for unmarked police cars, you three behind! It always strikes me as strange how much less this car vibrates at eighty than at seventy. Something to do with hitting the natural frequency of the bodywork, I understand . . . and over eighty it just seems to float . . . Yes, I shall try to avoid driving in France! I must admit I always used to find it terribly frightening, everything coming straight at you on the wrong side of the road. Stop gripping the dashboard, Ruth! There is no need! Although I must point out it is a sign that you are improving already. Yesterday you didn't care whether you died or not . . ."

As they neared the south coast the weather grew worse. They drove through rain squall after rain squall while the buffeting wind grew stronger and stronger. At the ferry port people were huddled under the shelter of buildings, watching the water. Small choppy waves slapped at the harbor walls. Close by, dozens of little yachts dipped and swung.

None of this meant anything at all to the girls. Even when they were aboard and Phoebe pointed out the red-coated stewards hurriedly restocking wire racks with sea-green paper sick bags, they did not grasp what was in store for them. The only thing that alarmed them was the voices of the crew as they chatted to one another.

"They're speaking French *already*!" hissed Naomi.

"It's a French ship," said Big Grandma. "I think we should go on deck."

"Why?"

"I always like to know exactly where the lifeboats are," said Big Grandma.

The last of the cars was loaded onboard, the gangway was trundled aside, the final cable unfastened, and the ferry was under way. At first it moved so slowly that the girls still felt part of the life that was going on ashore. After that they went through a period of agreeing that they could still swim back if they had to, and it was a comforting thought. But suddenly the last of England was slipping away very fast. It was greenish, grayish bumps. It was a low, smoky shadow. And then it was gone. Big Grandma, Phoebe noticed, had never once looked back to England from the moment she stepped on board. Her eyes were on the far horizon, even though she had warned them herself that France was hours and miles away.

She is very eager to get there, thought Phoebe, and wondered why and if Big Grandma could possibly be an international spy herself. It would certainly explain the scrap of conversation she had overheard on Thursday night. ". . . taking Rachel and Phoebe *as well?*" and then ". . . *Excellent cover?* Oh, company! Cover, I thought you said . . ." Perhaps she *had* said that, thought Phoebe, who would much rather be excellent cover than excellent company any day.

"All right, Phoebe?" called Big Grandma. "Want to go inside?"

"No, thanks," said Phoebe, discovering all at once that she quite dreadfully did not want to go inside.

"Come and sit by me."

Phoebe got to her feet and tottered toward her. The deck seemed to be taking an unkind delight in slapping the soles of her feet as she stepped. She reached Big Grandma, collapsed into the seat beside her, and put her head in her lap.

I don't feel much like cover, she thought dolefully, and fell asleep.

Naomi sat on the step of a roped-off staircase leading to the upper deck and tried to read Housman. Her mind would not concentrate. Nothing made sense. Over and over again she read the same meaningless verse:

> *The toil of all that be*
> *Helps not the primal fault*
> *It rains into the sea,*
> *And still the sea is salt.*

It was raining into the sea now, and the taste of salt was everywhere and the surge and pull of the waves exactly matched the surge and pull of Naomi's lurching stomach. *The only way to survive,* she thought grimly, *is to pretend Mr. Blyton-Jones is standing directly behind me.*

Rachel was having a marvelous time. She had been dispatched by Big Grandma in search of sea-green paper bags and, finding all the racks mysteriously empty, had gone on to discover a completely deserted restaurant. Six admiring waiters took turns to serve her large helpings of everything she pointed to. She had hot onion soup, roast chicken, spaghetti bolognese, two puddings, three milk shakes, and a glazed apple tart. It cost her her whole week's spending money, but Big Grandma, she told herself, would certainly provide a refund.

"It's only lunch," she said to a passing waiter. "I have to eat something." And he nodded to show that he quite agreed.

Like Naomi, Ruth was attempting to distract her thoughts with literature, but for the first time in all her many readings of *Jane Eyre* she found no comfort in Mr. Rochester. Her sympathies were suddenly all with Jane.

"Horrible, horrible abroad!" she gulped. "No wonder she didn't want to go! When I get off this terrible boat, I shall never leave dry land again!"

"You'll have to if you want to get home," Naomi replied, breathing deeply between each word. "That's what I keep thinking. How will we ever get home?"

Ruth groaned and turned back to Mr. Rochester, who was busy trying to persuade poor Jane to leave Thornfield for a whitewashed villa on the shores of the Mediterranean with no mention at all of how she was to get there.

I don't know what I ever saw in him, thought Ruth miserably, and at that moment Naomi stopped trying to pretend any longer that Mr. Blyton-Jones was witnessing her torment, and rushed to grasp the rails. At the sight Ruth gave up her own battle against the inevitable and lurched to join her.

"Not *into* the wind!" called Big Grandma, but was too late.

❦ ❦ ❦

That was the worst part of the journey. An hour later the wind had dropped, Rachel had reappeared and fetched paper towels, a new horizon was in sight, and a white-faced passenger had been clearly heard to remark that she had crossed the Channel four times a year for the last twenty-two years and had never known such a swell. Mr. Rochester was gone; he had tumbled overboard shortly after Ruth and Naomi had found the right side on which to be sick. There had been a flutter of white paper, a brief crimson stain in the churning water below, and no more.

"Poor Jane," said Ruth. "Just what she didn't want to happen."

The car journey that followed the ferry crossing had the heavy, endless character of travel in a dream. Hopelessly lost, exhausted, and ravenous, the girls dozed and woke and slept again through mile after mile of gray French countryside. When they later tried to recall those first few hours, they found that none of them could tell exactly where their swaying consciousness ended and where their jerking dreams began.

Ruth found herself waking at the roundabouts and unaccountably remembering her bus driver.

Why now? she thought sleepily. *Isn't this holiday supposed to cure me of being in love?* What did school bus drivers do over the holidays? she wondered. Did they dream of their passengers when they slept? What was the point of crossing the English Channel diagonally at one of its widest points if the faces of the people she was endeavoring to forget appeared as vividly as life the minute dry land was reached?

Not a very good start, thought Ruth morosely, and fell asleep again.

Naomi slumped uncomfortably in the front seat and dreamed of Housman. She came around to find that the light had gone and they were apparently on the brink of driving into black water. A wave of panic flooded over her before she woke up enough to realize that the car had stopped. They were on a harbor's edge. Big Grandma was poring over a map.

"I can't *think* what's happened to the roads," she muttered peevishly. "Oh, are you awake, Naomi?"

"Yes."

"There should be a bridge. There always *was* a bridge."

"Are we lost?"

"Don't be ridiculous," said Big Grandma, jerking the car into motion with terrifying suddenness, "and don't scream when I'm trying to reverse!"

Naomi stared meaningfully at the waiting blackness that now seemed even closer but prudently did not reply.

"There was a post," said Big Grandma, sparing a moment to follow her gaze when they were back on the comparative safety of the road.

"I didn't scream," said Naomi. "It was you."

"What?"

"You screamed. How long is it since you were here before?"

It was not until she was nearly asleep again that she heard the reply.

"Twenty-five years."

Rachel did not wake. In her sleep she fumbled constantly with the adjustment of her crown.

Phoebe was the only one alert enough to notice when they finally arrived. For quite a while she had been half-awake, and had been sleepily aware of the fact that Big Grandma's driving had become faster and faster as the journey progressed. At first when the car stopped she still kept her eyes tight shut, unwilling to leave the foggy safety of sleep, and expecting any moment to hear Big Grandma command them into action. Surprisingly no order came. There was a crunch of gravel beneath the wheels, the silence of the engine, a quiet click, and a sudden draft of cold air.

She's climbed out, thought Phoebe. She opened her eyes and just for a moment thought she was still dreaming. Big Grandma appeared to have turned into an enormous blue man. Phoebe rubbed her eyes again, the image disentangled, Big Grandma materialized again, but the blue man was still there. He was holding both of Big Grandma's hands and pumping them up and down. There was no sound at all but the rustle of wind through invisible leaves.

"In the old days," said Big Grandma severely, "it was at the far end of the orchard and no one complained!"

The blue man had gone. Phoebe had hurriedly closed her eyes again as he bent to peer through the car windows, but she had heard Big Grandma's whispered introductions.

"Ruth. Naomi. Rachel . . ."

"Ah!" said the blue man.

"And Phoebe."

Phoebe, squinting cautiously through her eyelashes, saw a square of yellow in the darkness. Somewhere in a house a light had been switched on. At the sight of it the blue man said, "Ah!" again, straightened up, and hurried away. With his vanishing the French cure for the family failing began.

One by one they stumbled into the cold night air and gazed around. In front of them was a long, low cottage. All around were trees, shadowy and gleaming with a pale whiteness.

"Apple trees," said Big Grandma, and they realized that the whiteness was apple blossom.

A field's distance away were the dark shapes of buildings, an enormous barn and the house where Phoebe had noticed the light.

"But it's gone," she said.

"What has?"

"There was a light."

"I expect they've closed the shutters," said Big Grandma. "All French houses have shutters on their windows. Very sensible."

The cottage had shutters, too, on every window, and they were all closed. Inside, floors, walls, and ceilings were entirely lined with wood. It smelled of a million dinners. It had no bathroom, or so they thought until Big Grandma led them out of the back door, around the corner past the kitchen windows, and up to a black-painted shed.

Inside was an enormous toilet, two steps up on a sort of miniature stage, an equally enormous hand basin, a framed picture of the English royal family at Sandringham, and, in the place where the light switch should have been, a huge black flashlight on a string. It was not a pleasant place. Even Big Grandma's remarks about what might have been worse at the end of the apple orchard did not make it seem any better. Nobody was very impressed, nobody except Rachel, that is. Rachel, seated on that most thronelike of conveniences, still wearing her crown and with the house of Windsor for company, felt perfectly at home.

"The first thing to do," announced Big Grandma, "is to get the car unloaded so that I can put it away."

"Is there a garage?"

"It goes in the barn."

"Why can't it stay outside?"

"Because Madame Carodoc likes things to be tidy. Very tidy, if I remember rightly."

"She won't like us, then," remarked Naomi.

"I don't suppose she'll see much of you," said Big Grandma as she passed bags out of the trunk. "It's Monsieur Carodoc who takes care of the cottage."

"Was he the blue man?" inquired Phoebe.

"Oh," said Big Grandma, looking suddenly rather put out. "I thought you were asleep."

"I saw a blue man," said Phoebe. "Just as I woke up. Blue trousers and a blue sweater and a blue hat."

"Blue hair?" asked Naomi, although without much hope, because it would be asking too much to have come to a place where complete blueness was the natural state of affairs.

"No," said Phoebe firmly. "Not blue hair. But enormous."

"Yes, well, that would be Charles," said Big Grandma.

"What on earth are these huge bags? I'm sure I didn't put them in."

"Just things," said Ruth, grabbing the nearest of them hastily.

"Stuff we didn't want to leave behind."

"What sort of stuff?"

"Books," said Naomi.

"And clothes," added Phoebe.

"Pictures and projects," said Rachel.

"Not that rubbish your mother thought she'd thrown away?"

"Martin rescued it," explained Phoebe, "and smuggled it all back to us, and we thought we'd better bring it with us in case it got thrown away again while we were gone."

"Well, I must admit I'm all for second chances," said Big Grandma cheerfully. "Take it inside while I put the car away. You can be choosing your beds."

There was one bedroom on the ground floor and two more at the top of a polished wood staircase that was as slippery as ice. The rooms opened out from a dark, windowless corridor, but there was a communicating door between the two.

"And no bunk beds," said Rachel happily. "I like this place!"

"It smells terrible."

"Just of cooking. Anyway, we can open the windows."

That seemed a good idea. They found the catches and pushed back the shutters, and the cold, sweet smell of apple blossom poured into the rooms.

"You see," said Rachel. "It's lovely!"

The first thing Big Grandma did on returning from parking the car was fall down the stairs. It was a spectacular descent; a skidding, careening plunge from top to bottom, and afterward the girls agreed that she could not possibly have done it on purpose. And yet when the thunderous thudding was over, the shrieks had died down, the injured had staggered to a chair and inspected her rapidly blackening shins and swelling right ankle, there was a definite note of triumph in her voice when she announced, "No getting about for me for a while!"

Chapter Seven

"RACHEL LIKED FRANCE, right from the beginning."

"She was the only one that did!"

"Do you remember the apple orchard all in blossom where Big Grandma took root!"

"And the cottage! And the creaks and the shadows and Madame Carodoc in her dressing gown!"

"Poor Madame Carodoc; she didn't like us very much."

"Not very much."

"I am hungry," said Rachel pathetically, late that first foreign evening. "Starving. Aren't we ever going to have any food?"

"Food?" asked Naomi. She had almost forgotten about food. The last meal she had eaten had been the dawn-time breakfast in England. It seemed very far away and long ago now, as remote as a dream.

"It's much too late to eat," said Ruth.

"Rubbish!" contradicted Big Grandma from the sofa, where she was comforting her swollen ankle with duty-free brandy. "Of course you must have a meal! Charles said he'd go shopping for us. Go and have a hunt in the kitchen."

The hunt in the kitchen turned out to be reasonably rewarding, even though a lot of Monsieur Carodoc's shopping consisted of what Ruth described as "ingredients": eggs and raw steak and onions and similar problems. But there was also bread and butter, tomatoes, and a cooked chicken. Big Grandma had brought tea bags and Phoebe discovered a kettle. Food was very reviving. After a while it began to seem that they might even summon sufficient strength to crawl upstairs to bed. Even Naomi cheered up enough to point out that after this night there would only be six more before they could go home. France began to look possible after all.

"There's a face at the window," said Phoebe quietly. Something in her voice gave her listeners a sudden sensation of ice-cold water trickling down their spines. They stared at her in horror, all except Big Grandma, who turned at once to the window.

"Nonsense!" she said immediately. "Not a soul!"

"There was a face," insisted Phoebe.

Big Grandma sighed but heaved herself to her feet, hobbled to the back door, and threw it open.

"No one!"

"A white face," persisted Phoebe. "Pale, like the apple blossom looks."

"You're just terribly tired," said Big Grandma. "I expect it was apple blossom."

"It was someone. It was a person."

"What sort of person? Old? Young? Sad? Laughing?"

"Watching," said Phoebe.

"You might wait till morning before you start discovering ghosts!"

"I didn't say it was a ghost."

"What, then?"

"I expect it was a spy, or someone like that. This *is* France!"

A spy was so typical of Phoebe that Ruth and Naomi, who had been looking very tense, immediately burst out laughing. Rachel, who had frozen midbite, sighed with relief and began chewing again.

"I'd completely forgotten Phoebe's preoccupation with spies," said Big Grandma cheerfully. "Bedtime as soon as you finish that chicken leg, Rachel!"

"Don't you believe me?" demanded Phoebe.

"Of course we do," said Big Grandma. "I expect there are secret agents behind every apple tree. Just stack the plates up for tonight. They can be washed in the morning."

"You'll be jolly sorry you didn't listen to me when you're murdered in your beds," said Phoebe crossly.

"We did listen to you," said Ruth yawning enormously. "Oh, I am tired! The worst thing about going to bed is having to visit the Black Hole first."

"The fuss you people are making about walking three steps past a lighted window!" Big Grandma exclaimed. "Go on and get it over with! Phoebe, if you're really feeling nervous, you can sleep with me tonight. It's a big double bed. I could easily squash you in."

Phoebe replied ungratefully that if it was a choice of sleeping with Big Grandma or being murdered in her bed, then she would undoubtedly prefer the latter fate.

"Especially," she added, having considered the matter further during her sojourn in the Black Hole, "since they will get you first because your room is downstairs."

"Charming," remarked Big Grandma. "Oh, well, good night. Rachel, if you have nightmares, it serves you right. I told you to leave that cheese alone. Take it off her, someone, and then upstairs, all of you. Don't be surprised if you hear a few creaks in the night, by the way. It'll just be the wood settling down."

"A few creaks!" groaned Naomi in the middle of the night. The darkness was full of noise; it sounded like the tuning up of some nightmare orchestra. Outside, the wind had risen and the shutters were thudding. Inside was even worse. Every single board of the wood-lined rooms twanged and creaked. Water pipes knocked. Rafters groaned. Rachel alone managed to sleep, snuffling and muttering, deep in cheese dreams, while her sisters lay awake and marveled that they had ever taken inside plumbing for granted. It became necessary to visit the Black Hole again and the corridor seemed endless, the stairs treacherous, and the night impossible.

"I really did see a face at the window," said Phoebe.

"Shut up," said Ruth.

Never had the royal family at Sandringham looked more aloof, and not even Ruth could summon up any interest in the spiders that the wavering light of the huge black flashlight revealed.

"I don't know why we ever came to this horrible abroad," she remarked morosely on the journey back, and Big Grandma, lying awake in the downstairs bedroom, overheard and for a moment almost agreed.

"Family failing," replied Naomi. "This is Big Grandma's surefire cure."

"I don't know how she knows anything about it. She's far too old! And even when she was much, much younger, can you imagine her ever having had it herself?"

Yes, I do know why I've come! Big Grandma told herself firmly. *And I'm not that ancient!*

"Anyway, if anything awful does come, they're sure to find her first, and we'll hear the screams and be able to climb out the window."

Phoebe! exclaimed Big Grandma to herself. *Callous little beast!* And she poured herself another dose of duty-free ankle medicine.

But I think I can guess what she saw, she thought. *My poor enemy.* And then, just as she finally fell asleep, she said suddenly aloud: "Or am I the poor enemy?"

"Was that a scream?" asked Phoebe, but nobody else had heard.

"It's certainly pretty," admitted Naomi, slightly grudgingly.

A flood of late-morning sunshine was pouring in the window. Monsieur Carodoc's land was on a small rise, so looking down from the bedroom Naomi and Ruth could see right over the tops of the pink and silver apple trees to rich green fields beyond. The whole landscape was crisscrossed with blossoming hedges. The air was full of the noise of birds, jubilant skylark music descending from the blue, finch and linnet song from the trees, and chickens on the ground. A mile or so away, looking like a line drawn with silver pencil between the fields and the sky, sparkled the sea.

"Pity it's French," remarked Naomi.

"The birds don't sound French," said Ruth. "They sound like proper English birds, even the chickens."

"Don't you remember how the chickens in Kenya spoke English?" asked Naomi. "I wonder what Joseck would say if he could see this?"

Joseck was their friend in Africa, a reference point in their lives. They had visited him once, and seen for themselves the hard, dry beauty of the Kenyan landscape, where every patch of growing green was a triumph. Recently Joseck had written that the rains in his district had been very small. It had not been a complaint, even though his family's fields depended upon the rain for survival; it had just been written as part of the news.

"Joseck would think it was Heaven," said Ruth, and she stopped complaining about the Frenchness of France, and went downstairs.

In the kitchen Rachel, Phoebe, and Big Grandma were busy consuming all but the most unapproachable of Monsieur Carodoc's supplies. Big Grandma, despite an ostentatiously bandaged leg propped up on a spare chair, looked very cheerful, and inquired kindly about the state of Ruth's sufferings under the family failing.

"A bit better," admitted Ruth, and felt herself turn crimson as she spoke. Since Thursday night neither she nor Naomi had mentioned the name of Mr. Blyton-Jones. The shame of having loved and lost to the charms of Fat-Slob-and-One-Leg was still too raw for either of them to discuss.

Nevertheless, it made one less to worry about, and Mr. Rochester, fathoms deep beneath the waves of the English Channel, made another. *Mr. Rochester is probably already disintegrating,* thought Ruth suddenly. After all, it had been a very old book.

"Two gone, anyway," she told Big Grandma.

"Well, every little bit helps," said Big Grandma, and tactfully did not inquire how many were still to go.

"Are we really here to cure Ruth of the family failing?" asked Phoebe. "It seems an awful long way to have to come to do it."

"Wait till it's your turn," Big Grandma told her. "We shall probably have to go round the world! Of course, it is also an excellent opportunity to blame Naomi's hairstyle on the French, and you will all be able to improve your foreign-language skills–don't look at me like that, Naomi–and you can learn to cook . . . Everyone has to learn sooner or later, Ruth; you might as well make up your mind to it . . ."

"I don't see why," said Ruth. "What's wrong with bread and cheese and apples and stuff out of cans?"

"And you will enjoy exploring the village," continued Big Grandma, ignoring this unsporting remark.

"I know what I was going to ask you," remembered Naomi suddenly. "Is there a church?"

"Of course. A very beautiful little stone-roofed one. Catholic, naturally."

"Has it got a graveyard?"

"What on earth do you want a graveyard for?"

"I was wondering if anyone had died here. It was jolly creepy last night."

"Yes, it was," agreed Phoebe, "and I *did* see a face."

Big Grandma looked suddenly irritated and began to demand that her granddaughters stop talking rubbish and scramble themselves some eggs. Rachel eagerly seconded this request and planted herself at the table to await a second breakfast, but Phoebe slipped outside to explore.

There's something strange about this holiday, she told herself as she wandered beneath the apple trees. *It's not just to cure Ruth of being in love, and Naomi's blue hair has nothing to do with it.* And she remembered again Big Grandma's headlong rush across France, and the strange, silent meeting with Monsieur Carodoc.

"And there *was* someone watching last night," she said. "I'm *not* obsessed with spies! There was. And I think Big Grandma knew there was, too." She decided to keep a careful eye on Big Grandma, just in case. In case of exactly what, she could not say, but at any rate it would be good spying practice, and Big Grandma might one day be grateful for her help. *After all*, thought Phoebe hopefully, *she does have a bad leg, and obviously could not get anywhere very fast, should she need to go anywhere very fast, that is.* And she had a sudden happy vision of a desperate car chase across the French countryside, Big Grandma in hot pursuit of the enemy. Or would the enemy in hot pursuit of Big Grandma be more exciting?

"We *are* just cover," said Phoebe aloud. "I knew we were!"

The first notable thing to happen that Sunday morning was the arrival at the cottage of Monsieur Carodoc, and when the girls saw him they knew at once the origin of Philippe's colossal charm. Monsieur Carodoc was Philippe all over again: the same illuminating smile, the same amused black eyes, and the same air of having known them for all of their lives. They loved him at once. It would have been impossible to do anything else; he was so welcoming, so miraculously one of the family, so enormous, and so blue. Also, he spoke perfect English. And even if he had had no other virtue, they would have loved him anyway because he told them he had come to cook their dinner.

"But first I must say *bonjour* and welcome," he announced and, starting with Phoebe and working up to Big Grandma, shook hands and kissed them all four times, twice on each cheek.

"Phoebe!" he said proudly. "Rachel! Naomi! Ruth! Big Grandma! You see, I know you all already! Am I not right?"

"Who told you?"

"Philippe, of course. He has talked of nothing else. Phoebe, who so kindly read him bedtime stories at night . . ."

"Spy stories," said Phoebe. "Do you always wear blue clothes?"

"Breton blue. But how do you know it is always?"

"I saw you when we came last night."

"Ah! Espionage already!"

"Yes, indeed," Big Grandma told him. "We have wasted no time!"

Monsieur Carodoc laughed and turned to Rachel. "Now, you are the little May Queen! I hope you have brought your crown, Rachel."

"Of course," said Rachel, beaming up at him. "Shall I fetch it?"

"*Mais oui!* At once. *Vite! Vite!* What a smiling face!"

"If there's one thing Rachel likes," Naomi remarked, "it's being asked to wear her crown!"

"Naomi the poet, of course," said Monsieur Carodoc, twinkling at her cheerfully. "But why did Philippe not tell us of your beautiful hair?"

"It wasn't like this when he was in England," Naomi explained. "And not many people think it's beautiful."

"Here they will," Monsieur Carodoc assured her. "It is charming! It shines like flames! And now, lastly, this is Ruth, who loves hedgehogs and hates to cook! Oh, yes, I saw your look when you heard you need not face the steak!"

"And this is Big Grandma," said Rachel.

"Big Grandma I know from many years," said Monsieur Carodoc. "*Ma chère Louise!*"

"Your *chère* Louise?" repeated Phoebe.

"Certainly, my *chère* Louise," said Monsieur Carodoc.

For the next two hours he completely took over, sweeping the girls outside to admire his chickens, pointing out local landmarks, arranging garden chairs in sheltered corners all over the apple orchard for the convenience of Big Grandma's bad leg, preparing vegetables, opening bottles, and answering questions. They learned that Philippe and his parents had paid a visit to the Carodocs' farm the day after he returned from England.

"To talk of you," said Monsieur Carodoc. "You have certainly enchanted my Philippe!"

"All of us, or just me?" asked Rachel.

"Are you not all enchanting?" asked Monsieur Carodoc, smiling at her.

"Rachel," explained Naomi, "asked poor Philippe to marry her and he didn't say he wouldn't."

"He didn't didn't say he wouldn't," contradicted Rachel. "He said he *would*. Enchanted, too, and without a gun."

"I've been looking forward to meeting Philippe," remarked Big Grandma, and there was a general sighing when Monsieur Carodoc explained that unfortunately today this would not be possible because on Sundays Madame Carodoc always drove the twenty kilometers to Philippe's house straight after church to have lunch and spend the day with him and his mother.

"Which is why I am free to cook for you now," he finished, flourishing an enormous black frying pan.

"Will Madame Carodoc tell Philippe that we are here?"

"Of course! Without doubt! I expect they will talk of nothing else, but you did not tell him yourselves?"

"We came away so quickly, we forgot," Ruth explained, watching as he lifted the steaks from the refrigerator. "Can I ask you something without you thinking I'm rude?"

"Certainly."

"Is it true that French people eat horses?"

"Do you suspect that I am about to feed you horse?"

"I only wondered."

"Well," said Monsieur Carodoc, "this is not horse, although horse is not so bad. You will enjoy French food. You must go shopping in the village tomorrow and see what you can find."

"Us?"

"Who else? Poor Big Grandma must rest."

"Quite right," agreed Big Grandma. "Apart from anything else, it will be excellent for their French."

"But we haven't got any French!"

Monsieur Carodoc said there was no need to worry about that. French translations for everything they might ever want to ask were written inside his barn all over the walls, a lifetime's collection of all that the English could not say.

"Not really?"

"*Vraiment,*" Monsieur Carodoc assured them, and after lunch took them across the orchard to the barn to see for themselves.

"We have many guests from England to visit the cottage," he explained while they gazed in amazement at the dozens of words and phrases chalked neatly on the walls and huge double doors. "You must feel free to consult my barn whenever you like, but please remember to close the doors when you leave. Otherwise the chickens come in. Madame Carodoc cannot abide the chickens coming into the barn."

That same day Ruth took another painful step on the road to recovery from the family failing. Monsieur Carodoc insisted that they telephone their parents to tell them of their safe arrival, and when it was Ruth's turn to speak to her mother, Mrs. Conroy suddenly remembered some news.

"That's what I was meaning to tell you!" she exclaimed. "Alan Adair!"

"Alan Adair," repeated Ruth, feeling her insides turn to water.

"Such a nice boy. I was talking to him yesterday."

"Were you?" asked Ruth faintly.

"He certainly cheers up that butcher's shop! Most artistic, he's made all new labels, color-coded, pink for pork, blue for beef, white with little daisies for lamb. And the sausages all in coils like pantomime snakes! He'd noticed that you were not at school at the end of last week and he asked after you straightaway. I knew you'd be pleased."

"Oh."

"He tells me he's given up that art school idea. His uncle has offered him a permanent job . . ."

"What!"

"Very sensible. After all, he can always keep painting for a hobby. And he has an aptitude . . ."

"He's going to be a butcher?"

"Yes, so he won't be going away . . ."

"What about his mountaineering? He was going to be a mountaineer as well!"

Ruth's insides were no longer water. They were congealing into a miserable lump.

"He didn't mention mountaineering. He seemed very pleased with himself, though. And he hoped you'd send him a postcard. He boned a chicken for me as nicely as anybody could . . ."

The lump in Ruth's stomach gave a sudden heave.

"So are you enjoying yourselves?"

"Oh, yes."

"And the Little Ones are behaving?"

"Yes, yes."

"Be good, then! Dad sends his love. Put Naomi on for a quick word; I want to ask her about her hair."

Ruth passed the telephone to Naomi and reeled back to the cottage.

"Whatever is the matter?" asked Big Grandma.

"Alan Adair."

"Your nice redheaded friend? The mountaineer? The artistic one?"

"He's going to be a butcher."

"What!"

"Alan Adair. He's going to be a butcher."

"Is that bad?"

"He had a place at art college."

"Oh, dear."

"He told Mum he'd changed his mind."

"Well," said Big Grandma as bracingly as she could. "There's nothing wrong with being a butcher! Plenty of very nice people are butchers!"

"He boned Mum a chicken," said Ruth, and burst into tears and cried and cried.

"Nobody laugh!" ordered Big Grandma.

Nobody felt in the least like laughing, although Rachel remarked that she didn't know what all the fuss was about anyway. After all, as she pointed out, Ruth may have been in love with Alan Adair, but Alan Adair had never shown the slightest interest in Ruth, unless his sudden desire for a postcard from France could be counted as interest.

"Anyway, Ruth wouldn't care if it was," said Naomi. "Because he didn't say anything about it until after he decided to turn into a butcher."

"Well, *I* think he will be a lovely butcher," said Rachel,

remembering the little bit of free sow belly. "I don't know why Ruth isn't pleased."

"Ruth is very nearly a vegetarian," said Naomi, "and anyway . . ."

"What?"

"Nothing," said Naomi, but it was not nothing. Until that afternoon Alan Adair's shining success had seemed as certain as their own. They had all been so sure that it was only a matter of time before their humdrum lives were transformed by talent and good fortune into careers of glittering achievement. Now suddenly a small chill wind from the future had blown into their lives. If Alan Adair, that golden boy, was to end up a butcher in his uncle's shop, what horrors might their own fates have in store? It did not bear thinking of.

Rachel had no fear of the future. She was going to marry Philippe in a long white dress (very much like her May Queen's dress), wearing a silver crown (almost exactly like her May Queen's crown), with plenty of diamonds but no bridesmaids because she had had enough of being one of a crowd of females. She confided these plans to her sisters that evening while they were getting ready for bed.

"But of course," she told them graciously, pulling on her pajamas over her nice, warm, four-day-old underwear, "you can all come to the wedding."

Nobody seemed very grateful. Ruth replied that she didn't know if she wanted to waste an afternoon watching Rachel marry old Snail Omelette, and Naomi said, "You put that underwear on Wednesday night when Mum made you have a bath. I remember getting it out of the bureau for you."

"What's that got to do with my wedding?" asked Rachel. "I suppose I could have one bridesmaid. Phoebe. So people don't wonder why I haven't got any."

Phoebe, standing at the window pretending to ignore the conversation, thought fiercely, *I'd rather die*, and concentrated her attention on the scene below. Big Grandma was still outside. She had spent the day reading in the orchard, hobbling ostentatiously between the garden chairs and little tables that Monsieur Carodoc had set out for her, following the sun.

"Thank goodness Naomi brought all those books," she remarked. "Enough to last the whole week."

Monsieur Carodoc had been back and forth to the apple orchard all day. Phoebe could see him there still, in earnest conversation with Big Grandma. They looked exactly like international spies, she thought: the shadowy table piled with books, those two old figures, heads bent together, completely absorbed in their secrets.

Out of the corner of her eye she caught a slight movement, a little patch of darkness on the edge of the orchard. It hovered beneath the trees, appearing and disappearing against the blackness of their trunks.

"Come and look here!" Phoebe whispered urgently to her sisters, and at that moment Monsieur Carodoc stretched and rose to go.

"What is it?"

"Something in the orchard."

"What sort of thing?"

"Black. Moving by the trees."

"You don't mean Monsieur Carodoc?" asked Rachel, yawning.

"Of course I don't. I can't see it now."

"More spies I suppose, then," said Ruth mournfully, too deflated by the dismal fate of Alan Adair to care very much. "There's Big Grandma coming in. Let's go and get the Black Hole over with before she comes inside and then she can stand guard."

She hurried out of the room and Rachel followed close behind her, but Naomi and Phoebe remained motionless at the window.

"Big Grandma's not limping half so much tonight," remarked Naomi.

"I did see someone," said Phoebe. "There! Look!"

For a moment the black shape had reappeared, far behind Big Grandma.

"Somebody watching," said Phoebe with satisfaction.

Chapter Eight

"FRENCH SHOPPING!"
"No Philippe!"
"And haunted!"
"And your hair!"
"My hair was quite a success."

"Well," said Big Grandma cheerfully when Ruth came down on Monday morning. "Three down now, Ruth! Do you feel any improvement in yourself?"

It was nice, decided Ruth, the way Big Grandma obviously considered the family failing to be an illness, bad luck, with no personal blame attached to the sufferer. It was like the difference between having spots and measles. Nobody said to the measled, "Do you wash? And what have you been eating? Junk? Chips and chocolate? You must have done something to get yourself in such a mess." Measles were random; they could strike anyone, it might one day be yourself . . . Big Grandma had many faults, thought Ruth, but she never forgot that it was no good blaming someone for their fate; one should shut up and be thankful to have escaped oneself.

When Rachel said that she didn't know how Ruth could possibly be in love with people who hardly knew she existed, Big Grandma said, "You're lucky then, Rachel! And don't speak too soon."

"*And* more than one at a time," continued Rachel.

"Numbers have nothing to do with it," said Big Grandma severely. "One does not count!"

Philippe and the bus driver, counted Ruth in her head. *Mr. Blyton-Jones and Mr. Rochester, gone without a trace. Alan Adair . . . Alan Adair was still very painful.*

"I think I'll turn into a vegetarian," she announced.

"Very sensible," said Big Grandma. "Join Phoebe. And, speaking of food, we'd better make a list. You girls will have to go shopping after breakfast."

"Aren't you coming?"

"With my ankle?"

"What will you do, then?"

"I shall sit quietly in the orchard with A *Tale of Two Cities*. I always enjoy books much more when I read them on location. But first, what do we need?"

"Bread," said Rachel immediately. "Butter, jam, eggs, more chicken, ham, cheese, cakes, apples, milk . . ."

"Trust you to know," said Big Grandma, busy scribbling. "Go on! Don't stop!"

"Tomatoes, lettuce, chocolate . . ."

Naomi sighed and Big Grandma guessed the reason.

"There is nothing to be afraid of," she said. "People will know you are English. They won't expect miracles. All you have to do is be polite . . . French people are much more polite than English."

"Crackers, potatoes, bananas . . ."

Rachel's list grew longer and longer. Her sisters left her to it and rushed across the apple orchard for a feverish consultation of the barn walls.

The first French person they met was not very polite at all.

The Carodoc house stood between the orchard and the barn. It had low, latticed windows and one of them was open.

"Are there snakes in France?" asked Phoebe when they emerged from the barn.

"Snakes?"

"Listen. And what's that knocking?"

The knocking was fierce and insistent, a bitter sound like stone on stone. It was coming from the house. A large bony hand showed at the window. A long yellow finger rapped hard on the glass.

"It must be Madame Carodoc."

"Is she doing it at us?"

"I suppose she must be."

"Why is she hissing?"

Ruth glanced helplessly around, noticed a chicken, and suddenly remembered. The barn door; they had forgotten it. She turned back and swung it shut and the rapping stopped, but not the hissing.

"She wants us to go over," said Naomi.

Madame Carodoc sat at a table at the open window.

"She looked like she was filling in a register," Naomi said afterward.

"Doing the accounts," said Big Grandma.

"She wasn't dressed."

"Don't be silly!"

"I mean she had a dressing gown on. Whitey, pinky, purpley cotton. All frills."

"A wrapper," said Big Grandma. "I'm sure I remember the very same one!"

"We said hello."

"*Bonjour*," they had called as they approached, nervously but smiling, one after the other. "*Bonjour! Bonjour!*"

Madame Carodoc did not say *bonjour*. Or smile. She snapped out something in French.

"*Où est l'autre?*"

They had not the faintest idea what she meant. She repeated it over and over again while they stared dumbly at each other, and then suddenly it clicked. Rachel! Where was Rachel? She was asking for Rachel. They turned to point at the cottage, and there, like a miracle, was Rachel herself, waving an enormous shopping list and running across the grass.

"Rachel!" they said, pointing. "Rachel! There!"

Madame Carodoc reached out and closed the window.

"She hates us!"

"Of course she doesn't," said Big Grandma. "She always was a little bit difficult. I'm afraid she just doesn't seem to like the English. I hope you weren't rude."

"*She* was rude!"

"You must have annoyed her. Try not to annoy her."

"We forgot to close the barn door; that was all."

"Well, don't forget again. That's easy enough."

"I shall tell Philippe what I think of his horrible grandmother," said Phoebe.

"I hope he doesn't tell you what he thinks of yours," laughed Big Grandma.

Naomi read Housman all the way into the village. Housman always gave her a sort of courage; it was something to do with the way he didn't appear to care about anything. Death was the only thing that seemed to matter much to Housman.

"All Housman's friends were dead," said Naomi.

"People are looking at your hair," said Ruth.

Naomi glanced up in surprise and realized that while she had been engrossed they had arrived in the middle of the village. She saw shops and houses facing onto an enormous cobbled marketplace, a crumbling statue of a horse and rider, and four huge chestnut trees, one at each corner of the square. Ruth was right, people *were* looking at her hair.

"They needn't stare!" she whispered, and was about to continue, "Haven't they ever seen a person with blue hair before?" when she realized that they probably hadn't.

"Do you think they know we're English?" she asked instead.

"Yes," replied Ruth gloomily. "And even if they don't, they soon will. They know we're something funny already. You can tell by their faces. Do I look scared?"

"A bit. Do I?"

"No," admitted Ruth. "But no one with blue hair *could* look really scared. Where've Rachel and Phoebe got to?"

"I'm here," said Phoebe from behind. "And Rachel's in the middle of that crowd."

They looked where she was pointing and saw to their dismay that Rachel was disgracing them already. She had discovered the *pâtisserie* and immediately (having no shame) emptied her pockets to see what she could afford. Passers-by had stopped to help her count francs and centimes and translate them into tarts and pastries. From across the other side of the square her sisters could hear French voices and laughter mingled with shrill, and unmistakably English, squeals of admiration and greed.

"How many would I get of *that* one, then?" they heard her demand over and over again as she pointed to each new temptation behind the plateglass window, and then there would be a period of heavy breathing and tension while her audience inspected her sticky handful of money and pronounced the result.

"Oh, I wish Philippe was here!" exclaimed Ruth in despair.

"Philippe!" said Phoebe bitterly. "I don't believe he's ever coming."

"What *do* you mean? Oh, *look* at beastly Rachel! Someone's gone in and bought her something."

"Let's sneak back to the cottage and leave her," suggested Naomi.

"We can't," said Ruth reluctantly. "Come on. I can see a fruit shop. Let's go and get it done with while the crowds are still all over there."

The fruit shop was a disaster. Once again they got as far as the smiles and *bonjours*, but the trouble was that people replied to them when they spoke. If only they had shut up and listened carefully, things might have been possible. In school French lessons they could ask for apples and tomatoes with no trouble at all, but then nobody interrupted. Nobody in school French was unreasonable enough to say, "Which apples? Can you wait while we unpack some fresh? Ten kilos? No, I can't sell you ten kilos and you couldn't carry them home if I did. Two will be plenty. Ripe potatoes? Oh, tomatoes. Very ripe or a little green? No, not blue, a little green. Where are you from and would you like a bag? Do you like France and who is the eldest?"

It was dreadful. It was like being under siege, and most terrible of all was the moment in the middle of the onslaught when Ruth's treacherous memory suddenly recalled a phrase of perfect French and to her horror she heard herself shouting, "*Taisez-vous! Taisez-vous! Taisez-vous!*" There was a horrible silence. Exactly the sort of dreadful quiet that would arise in an English shop if, in response to the good-natured helpfulness of the shop-keeper, some unknown and undoubtedly ignorant foreigner screeched, "Shut up! Shut up! Shut up!"

"Stop it!" exclaimed Naomi furiously to Ruth. "Stop it! Stop it!"

"It's the *wrong* thing to say!" said Phoebe.

Ruth knew perfectly well that it was the wrong thing to say; she had known it before she opened her mouth to speak, but she was panicking now and could not stop.

"*Taisez-vous!*" she continued to bleat as her sisters shoved her out of the door. "*Taisez-vous! Taisez-vous!*"

"You deserve to be *killed!*" said Naomi.

"*Taisez-vous*," whispered Ruth one more time, and shut up.

While Ruth, crimson with shame and wilting with misery, sat hunched on a seat under a chestnut tree and guarded the bags of apples and tomatoes that had been thrust into her arms, Naomi and Phoebe found what in England would have been a very glorious delicatessen, and in France was the *charcuterie*.

The window display was most enticing.

"It sells nearly everything on the list," said Phoebe.

"I suppose it does."

"Are you scared?"

"Of course I am."

"They can't actually *do* anything to us!"

"Come on, then," said Naomi, and pushed open the door.

Two minutes after they had entered the shop she shot out of the doorway as if she had been kicked.

"I'm sure they're just doing it to be nasty!" she said, flinging herself down beside Ruth.

"What?"

"All this talking in French at us."

"Did they do it again?"

"As soon as we got in."

"What happened?"

"I thought this time I would try to explain things right from the start so I said, '*Bonjour*. I am English. I don't understand any French unless it is written down in the present tense.' I thought I could manage to understand if they would do that."

"Then what?"

"As a matter of fact," said Naomi stiffly. "They started swearing. So I came away."

Quite by accident Phoebe discovered the secret of French shopping.

When Naomi had fled from the battlefield, Phoebe had remained rooted to the spot, and while on that spot she had had a thought: *Do not speak,* Phoebe had warned Phoebe. *It is saying* bonjour *that sets them off.*

She assumed what she hoped was an expression of hunger, plonked a handful of notes and ten-franc pieces onto the counter, and stepped backward to stare silently at the floor.

Slowly, at first, and then faster and faster the magic began to work. The two assistants behind the counter seemed suddenly to become quite desperate to sell. One of them came out and with a gentle arm around Phoebe pointed questioningly to all that she guessed Phoebe might want to purchase, while the other, cleverly judging the quantity required from the distance Phoebe showed them between her hands, cut and weighed and wrapped. As the pile of purchases grew on the counter, the atmosphere became happier and happier. Phoebe changed her expression of despair to one of slight hope and they beamed at her in encouragement. She allowed herself to smile and they whacked her on the back in congratulation. She began to point herself to what she required and they embraced her on both cheeks. Under a storm of compliments she took her change, nodded her thanks, staggered victoriously out into the street, and bumped straight into Rachel.

Rachel was equally laden and smeared from the waist upward in apricot tart.

"I think France is fantastic," she told Phoebe happily.

"I'm never going into the village again," said Ruth.

"Of course you are," replied Big Grandma unsympathetically. "It's all part of the cure."

Big Grandma was in the highest of spirits that lunchtime, despite her bad leg (which, judging from her groans and limping, seemed to be growing worse by the hour). She had roared with laughter at the girls' description of the hideous shopping expedition, and had not even complained when it was discovered that Phoebe's purchases included fondant chocolates ("I don't remember pointing to them," said Phoebe) and a beautiful terrine of truffle pâté. ("Yes, I do remember pointing to that. I had to point *hard*. They didn't seem to want to sell it.")

It was a very delicious lunch.

"Next time will be easier," said Big Grandma. "And you really needn't have got into such a muddle. People would have been glad to help you if they'd understood."

"Madame Carodoc was in that first shop," Ruth told her. "She understood all right, but she didn't help."

"Is that where she was this morning?" said Big Grandma. "Charles said she had gone out."

"She saw us and sneaked away. She thought we didn't see her."

"I'm sure she didn't."

"She laughed."

"Well, perhaps you were funny."

"I liked shopping," said Rachel comfortably. "Everyone was nice to me. Next time if they like, the others can stay at home and I'll just go with Philippe."

"Philippe!" exclaimed Big Grandma. "That's what I meant to tell you. Apparently he has flu!"

"Flu!"

"Madame Carodoc told Charles that he was quite poorly when she saw him yesterday."

"Nobody has flu in May!"

"So I'm afraid you can't expect to see him for a day or two yet."

There was a dismayed silence around the table.

Oh, poor girls! thought Big Grandma at the sight of their stricken faces. *Poor girls! But surely not all four . . . I knew about Rachel, of course, and I suspected that Ruth . . .*

"I'm sure he'll come as soon as he can," she said kindly, because although the agonies of French shopping might leave her unmoved, she was always considerate to those afflicted with the family failing. "I'm sure he'll come. Monsieur Carodoc says he's often over here during the holidays . . ."

"Flu in May," said Naomi in scorn.

"I didn't think he'd turn up," said Phoebe bitterly. "I thought he was just pretending to like us."

"Oh, Phoebe!"

"He wasn't pretending with me," said Rachel cheerfully. "He couldn't have been or he wouldn't have said he'd marry me. Can I finish off that truffle stuff if nobody else wants it?"

"That's the spirit!" said Big Grandma, pushing the pâté

toward her. "Of course he wasn't pretending! Charles says he thought you were all wonderful. You're just depressed because you've had a horrible morning. Do something nice this afternoon. Take a picnic and go to the sea."

"The sea?" asked everyone. They had forgotten about the sea.

"There's a lovely beach not much more than twenty minutes' walk away. We used to see lizards on the rocks there, I remember, and your mother loved it because of the shells. There's a map book in the car with the local roads shown . . ."

"What about you?" asked Ruth. "Won't you be lonely?"

"No," said Big Grandma.

"Don't you get bored?"

"Only people with no mental resources get bored."

"Does Madame Carodoc come to talk to you?" asked Phoebe.

"Madame Carodoc?" asked Big Grandma. "No. Why should she?"

"Well, Monsieur Carodoc does."

"No," said Big Grandma, looking suddenly irritated. "No, she doesn't. Madame Carodoc and I have very little in common."

Phoebe thought she could name one thing they had in common, but a warning glint in Big Grandma's eyes made her decide not to mention it.

"Shall I get the map book?" asked Rachel.

"Go on, then," said Big Grandma, relaxing a little. "It's in the glove compartment. And don't forget . . . Oh, she's gone without even waiting for the key! Run after her quickly, Phoebe, and tell her not to forget to close up the barn. No point in annoying anyone . . ."

The door slammed again as Phoebe followed after Rachel. ". . . unnecessarily," said Big Grandma.

Unnecessarily or not, it seemed that Madame Carodoc was determined to be annoyed. Rachel and Phoebe had hardly turned from shutting the heavy barn door before she was out of the house, pushing past them to check that they had properly fastened the latch. Phoebe muttered an unen-thusiastic, "*Bonjour,* Madame Carodoc," and moved away as invisibly as she knew how, but Rachel, who so far had not encountered their hostess, stood dopily waiting to be greeted and thanked.

No greetings came, so Rachel said, as she had been say-ing all morning, "*Bonjour. Je suis Rachel. Ça va?* That means how are you, and then you say, '*Ça va*' back."

The people outside the *pâtisserie* who had taught her this feat of fluency had been enchanted to hear it put into practice, but if Madame Carodoc was enchanted, she hid it very well. "Shoo! Shoo!" she exclaimed, scuttling past Rachel to clap her hands and shake her black skirts at a watching hen.

"Then when she'd chased the chicken she turned round and chased *me!*" recounted Rachel as they sprawled on the beach in the afternoon sunshine recovering from the effects of the picnic. "'Shoo! Shoo!' she said, just like I was a chicken, so I said, 'I'm not a chicken.'"

"I'm not a chicken," said Rachel, surprised but standing her ground. "Hasn't Philippe told you about me? Don't you speak any English? Monsieur Carodoc does. He cooked our dinner yesterday. I love French food!"

Madame Carodoc, evidently realizing that Rachel was not going to shoo, paused and stood looking at her.

"And how is your grandmother's leg?" she asked.

"Madame Carodoc said *that?*" asked Naomi incredulously.

"Yes. I thought you told me she didn't speak English."

"We didn't think she did!"

"Well, she does. And I told her Big Grandma was making an awful fuss about her leg but we thought it wasn't half as bad as she made out and she just liked making us do all the work while she sat about in the apple orchard."

"Did Madame Carodoc understand all that, then?"

"I don't know. I suppose so. She asked me why Big Grandma had brought us here and I said to cure Ruth of the family failing and so that we could blame Naomi's blue hair on the French but that Phoebe says that's all rubbish and we're just here for cover."

"And then what?"

"She went back into the house," said Rachel.

It was late afternoon when they left the beach and dusk by the time they returned to the cottage, laden with shells, salt-blown and staggering with sleepiness from the combined effects of sea air, food, and emotion. Big Grandma was in her usual place, and so was Monsieur Carodoc and so was the ghost. Naomi saw it at once, but by the time the rest turned to look where she was pointing, it had vanished among the shadows.

"*Bonsoir! Bonsoir!*" called Monsieur Carodoc, spotting

them and hurrying across the damp grass. "I was just about to come and meet you. You stayed late, you know; poor Big Grandma was worrying."

"Sorry," said Ruth. "But we were only just up the road. There are glowworms all under the hedges. We've never seen them before. Rachel wanted to collect some."

"And I saw a ghost," said Naomi.

"Non! Non! Non!" exclaimed Monsieur Carodoc. "That will frighten the little ones, Naomi! No ghosts in my orchard if you please!"

Right, thought Naomi, *that proves it. There is something and you know it. I never said anything about the orchard.*

"No frightening the little ones with ghosts," repeated Monsieur Carodoc firmly. "Whatever is your May Queen trying to do?"

Rachel had fetched her crown from the cottage and, watched disapprovingly by Ruth, was trying to persuade a party of glowworms to climb aboard and shine.

"They keep falling off," she complained as once again she tried to stand up and the glowworms from her crown tumbled like stars at her feet and disappeared into the darkness. "Why do they do that? Where do they go?"

"Don't move or you'll tread on them," warned Ruth. "They don't go anywhere. You just can't see them anymore."

"But are they still there?"

"Of course they are. How could they vanish?"

Other things vanish, thought Naomi while her sisters slept that night. There was a definite feeling of unease in the air. No Philippe was part of it. Big Grandma's air of remoteness, Madame Carodoc's obvious resentment, the dark figure in the apple orchard, Phoebe's face at the window. Not to mention the eeriness of the cottage at night.

Haunted! Haunted! Haunted! shouted Naomi's silent thoughts.

Chapter Nine

"I wish Monsieur Carodoc was here."

"Oh, Ruth!"

Very early on Tuesday morning Monsieur Carodoc arrived at the cottage and announced that he was taking them to the cliffs at the end of the world.

So Philippe can't be coming today, thought Ruth and, glancing across the table, saw exactly the same realization in Naomi's eyes. Although it had never been said in words, it was perfectly obvious that no one except Monsieur Carodoc and Rachel really believed that Philippe was incapacitated by flu.

And the fuss we made of him! thought Ruth. It almost made her cringe to think of the fuss that had been made of Philippe in the Conroy house. *If he doesn't come tomorrow . . .* she thought.

Naomi, to whom Philippe had only ever been a poor second to the fatal magnetism of Mr. Blyton-Jones, was already on the road to recovery. Phoebe, at the other extreme, was absolutely caustic. Only Rachel of the perfect faith was undisturbed. Rachel was completely happy in France. She didn't believe in ghosts, she was unembarrassed by her inability to speak the language, nothing in the way of French cuisine could shock her, and, best of all, thanks to Philippe, she was no longer the family grub. She was still glowing with the miracle of that transformation. Monsieur Carodoc said, "Rachel shines," and it was true.

Monsieur Carodoc's cliffs at the end of the world turned out to be the cliffs in south Finistère.

"It will be a long day," he warned.

"Hélène?" asked Big Grandma. "Will she come with us?"

"*Non, non*," said Monsieur Carodoc. "And, anyway, there wouldn't be room."

"We could take two cars."

"She still wouldn't come."

"If I went and asked her?"

"You might, I suppose," said Monsieur Carodoc, twinkling at Big Grandma. "You might hobble across and ask her. Or hop. Or perhaps the girls might carry you. It is not so very far, an arm or a leg each . . ."

"Don't be silly, Charles!"

"But she still wouldn't come."

"What if I stay behind? After all, I could never climb those cliffs."

"Don't be silly, Louise," said Monsieur Carodoc.

The cliffs were followed by a late and very long lunch at "a proper French restaurant," as Monsieur Carodoc said.

"Where real French people go?" asked Rachel.

"Exactly," said Monsieur Carodoc.

It was at the restaurant that Phoebe produced the only sentence of French that she was to attempt throughout the entire visit.

"Je ne manage pas les morts," said Phoebe, on being confronted with the menu, the chef, and the proprietor and his wife (all personal friends of Monsieur Carodoc). *"Je ne manage pas . . ."*

"Yes, thank you, Phoebe," interrupted Big Grandma. "That's quite enough French from you, vegetarian principles notwithstanding."

"Ah!" said Monsieur Carodoc, the chef, the proprietor and his wife. *"Végétarienne!"* And they looked at each other with raised eyebrows and faces that said, "Yes, well, English children. Nothing better to be expected."

Rachel saved them from disgrace.

"I wish," she said, after ages of drooling in indecision over the menu, "I could have a little bit of everything."

"Certainly you may have a little bit of everything," said Monsieur Carodoc at once. "Do you like melon?"

"Oh, yes, please!"

"Snails and mussels cooked together in herbs and butter?"

"I'm sure I would."

"Lobster with cream and tomatoes?"

"I like everything," said Rachel. "Even zebra."

She was a great success.

"No wonder," said Monsieur Carodoc as they drove back home, "that Philippe was so enchanted."

A moment before, all four girls had been fast asleep, but Philippe's name penetrated their dreams and everyone except Rachel was suddenly alert.

"I do hope we see Philippe soon," said Big Grandma. "The girls thought such a lot of him. I'm afraid they've been rather disap–"

"We haven't!" interrupted Ruth, Naomi, and Phoebe from the back.

"I thought you were all asleep!"

"Rachel is, that's all."

"I could telephone my malingering grandson and order him to his duty," suggested Monsieur Carodoc cheerfully. "I shall. I ought to and I shall!"

"Oh, no!" protested Naomi, and Ruth added, "Don't, Monsieur Carodoc! Oh, please don't! He will only think . . ."

"Well, so he should think," replied Monsieur Carodoc. "Breaking your hearts!"

"Please," begged Ruth. "*Please*, Monsieur Carodoc, don't telephone Philippe!"

"What, not tell him of your languishing?"

"We're *not* languishing!"

"Stop teasing them, Charles!" ordered Big Grandma. "Of course they are not languishing! If Philippe has flu, he has flu and that's all there is to it. Their hearts are quite intact."

"Well, shall I telephone to say their hearts are quite intact but still to come at once?"

"No!"

"That their hearts are quite intact and they don't care whether he comes or not?"

"No!"

"To say they just don't care?"

"No!"

There was never anyone, as the girls knew only too well, better at jumping to conclusions than Philippe. They could imagine the conclusion he would jump to if his grandfather informed him that they didn't care whether he came or not. They could almost hear his voice. "No?" Philippe would say, his eyes gleaming. "No?"

"Don't telephone *at all!*" said Naomi.

"Yes, Charles," agreed Big Grandma. "Mind your own business! They've all been having a wonderful time, isn't that true?"

"Except for the shopping," said Ruth.

"The shopping was nothing," said Big Grandma.

"The shopping was *terrible*," said Ruth.

"*Pourquoi?*" asked Monsieur Carodoc. "Tell me!"

Quite thankful to change the subject, Ruth told him, not leaving out anything, not even the disgraceful shouting of "*Taisez-vous!*"

"But I didn't really mean to," she explained. "It just came out. Their faces were awful!"

"I expect they just thought it was funny," said Big Grandma.

"I expect they didn't," said Monsieur Carodoc. "Poor girls! And poor, poor Ruth!"

"And you could see how dreadful they thought Naomi's hair!"

"Naomi's hair?" asked Monsieur Carodoc, obviously genuinely astounded. "But Naomi's hair is charming! Charming!"

"Is it?"

"Of course it is. And tomorrow you will all come shopping with me."

"Not into the village!"

"Certainly into the village. And you will see, everything will be quite all right."

Shopping in the village with Monsieur Carodoc was utterly different from shopping alone.

"I wish I knew what he said to them," said Naomi.

Whatever it was, it was very effective. The lady from the fruit shop abandoned a line of customers to come out and kiss Ruth. At the *charcuterie*, they said as soon as Naomi came in, "Ah, *bonjour! Bonjour!*" and, indicating her hair, "*Très, très jolie!*"

"I'm sure they didn't say that before," said Naomi when they were in the street again. "They were really nice!"

"And they understood our French!" marveled Ruth.

"Of course they did," said Monsieur Carodoc.

"And they didn't even mind what Phoebe said about the pâté!"

Phoebe, when asked whether she had enjoyed the truffle pâté, had once again produced her only sentence of French. This time it had brought down the house.

"So," said Monsieur Carodoc, "all there is to do now is rescue Rachel from the *pâtisserie*. Or perhaps I should say the *pâtisserie* from Rachel. Did I not tell you everything would be all right?"

"Three more nights," said Naomi on Wednesday evening.

Of all of them, Naomi was the one who minded the nights the most. Right from the start Rachel had always slept soundly; she didn't believe in ghosts or spies. Phoebe, although she watched Big Grandma as closely as ever, was also beginning to doubt the existence of international espionage in the apple orchard. Ruth's nights were still fairly busy with the rival claims of the bus driver and Philippe. Naomi, having recovered from Philippe and forsaken Mr. Blyton-Jones, was left with Housman for comfort, and Housman, read late at night by the light of an ancient and smelly oil lamp, was not comforting. He never shrank from reminding his readers in the plainest of language that they were not immortal.

> *Around the huddling homesteads*
> *The leafless timber roars,*
> *And the dead call the dying*
> *And finger at the doors.*

"This place *must* be haunted," Naomi had said the morning after the trip to the cliffs. The fingering on the door the preceding night had been beyond all reason.

"Too much rich food yesterday," said Big Grandma heartlessly.

Naomi was so unconvinced that she decided to pay a secret visit to the village graveyard. "To see who it might be," she explained to Ruth. "Won't you come?"

"No," said Ruth, who had a secret hope that Philippe might turn up that afternoon. "Don't go, Naomi. You won't find anyone, and, even if you did, what good could it do?"

Naomi did not know what good it could do, but she went anyway, and discovered that, far from finding no one, the choice was immense. Huge families of Carodocs seemed to have married and intermarried, raised dozens of children, and lasted into enormous old age before finally squashing down to rest among crowds of relations.

"What are you doing here?" demanded a voice in English, and Naomi spun around to see Madame Carodoc glaring at her.

"Just looking," she replied, very startled, and then, plucking up courage, "Madame Carodoc, is the cottage haunted?"

"Haunted?"

"Ghosts," explained Naomi.

"Ah, *ghosts!*" Madame Carodoc exclaimed, and laughed and laughed. "Not yet," she said.

"That wasn't very nice," said Ruth when Naomi told her the story. "Did she say anything else?"

"Only how was Big Grandma's leg that kept her sitting in the orchard for such a long, long time. I told her it was much better."

Big Grandma's leg did seem to be much better. She no longer spent her days reading in the apple orchard. Instead she drove them to local picnic spots that she remembered from years and years ago. She was very good at remembering them.

"I'd have thought everything would be changed," remarked Ruth.

"It has in a way," admitted Big Grandma. "Perhaps I shouldn't have come back."

Always at the end of the day Monsieur Carodoc

appeared. He and Big Grandma would sit together, talking and laughing and drinking wine.

"They don't look much like spies," said Phoebe disappointedly.

Still Philippe did not turn up.

Now it is too late, Ruth told herself on Wednesday night, and woke up on Thursday morning with one less on her family failing list.

"Getting better?" asked Big Grandma at breakfast time.

"Yes," said Ruth thankfully, although she was beginning to discover that falling out of love was a painful process. It had been bad enough with Alan Adair, but at least the end had come all at once, one gasp of shock and it had been over. Philippe had been much worse. All that waiting and hoping.

But even if he comes today, Ruth told herself, *it is too late. It is really too late.* And she said to Big Grandma, "Poor old Rachel."

"Yes, poor old Rachel," agreed Big Grandma.

Rachel was not at all unhappy. As far as she was concerned, Philippe had flu and could not come. Why else would he not come? Monsieur Carodoc had told them that Philippe knew quite well that he would drive over and fetch him any day he wished. He only had to telephone and ask. He had done it hundreds of times before.

"I am ashamed of him," Monsieur Carodoc said quite openly, when Rachel happened to be out of the way. "To treat his friends so! Say the word and I will tell him what I think of him!"

"Don't!" said Naomi and Ruth together.

"We don't want him if he doesn't want to come," added Phoebe. "Smarmy, smiling traitor! *Can* he read English?"

"Of course he can read English!" said Monsieur Carodoc, astonished. "Why?"

"I thought he must be able to when I saw you reading Big Grandma's paper," explained Phoebe. "If Philippe can read English, then I hate him! And that must mean he read all my dead-letter box notes, too! No wonder he knew so much about us!"

"Is that what you put in your dead-letter boxes?" asked Naomi. "Stuff about us?"

"That sort of thing," said Phoebe.

"But why?" asked Monsieur Carodoc, much amused to hear this revelation.

"Practice," said Phoebe, "for when I'm an international spy. I suppose I shall just have to start writing in code."

"You still plan to be an international spy?" asked Monsieur Carodoc.

"Of course," said Phoebe, although not quite so whole-heartedly as she would have done in the past. Somehow it no longer seemed quite such a desirable career, but perhaps it was only the thought of having to write everything in code that was so dampening.

No more was said about Philippe, but, as if to compensate, Monsieur Carodoc, who had always been kind, became even kinder, especially to Rachel. It was a time when everyone was being particularly nice to Rachel. There was something frightening about her contentment. It was like watching someone running toward a precipice, unaware of the drop. The drop was Philippe.

Philippe had changed so much for Rachel. He had made her confident. It had been a wonderful thing for Rachel to have someone consider her the best of all.

Madame Carodoc evidently considered her the worst of all.

"Not that she likes any of us," said Ruth, who had just been pounced on yet again.

"What did you do?"

"Barn door, as usual."

Ever since the disastrous shopping expedition, they had made up their minds that somehow or other they must manage to learn a bit more French. Monsieur Carodoc's barn walls were the easiest way of doing it, and the girls consulted them often. It drove Madame Carodoc mad. At the slightest rattle of the doors she came hurtling out of the house to mutter and fume and hustle the chickens. She said to the chickens what she would obviously have liked to say to her guests. "Go off! Go off! Nobody wants you here!" What was more, as the girls could not fail to notice, she said it in English.

"You would think it would be better to tell off a French chicken in French," remarked Naomi, earning herself an awful glare.

She took to tidying up after them. Tidying up to Madame Carodoc meant throwing in the trash can, or several trash cans. They would find their possessions disposed of in the most organized way, books in one can, sweaters in another.

"Well, French rubbish is all sorted out for recycling,"

said Big Grandma. "Much more sensible!"

"But I'd only left them outside for a minute!"

"Come on, Ruth," said Big Grandma. "It must have been more than a minute!"

"It was just while we went for lunch."

"It wasn't a minute, then," said Big Grandma reasonably. "This is Madame Carodoc's property. If you leave things lying about, you can't be surprised if they end up in the trash."

When Big Grandma was properly mobile and able to go out with the girls, things became even worse.

"Do you think she goes into the cottage?" demanded Naomi.

"Perhaps," said Big Grandma. "She probably likes to keep an eye on things."

"Our things!"

"Lots of people who rent out cottages go in to clean and tidy," said Big Grandma. "Anyway, we don't even know that she does."

It soon became obvious that she did.

"Rubbish to go outside!"

Ruth and Naomi, staggering back from the barn with their arms full of picnic things, stopped and stared.

"Rubbish *outside!*" repeated Madame Carodoc. "*Outside*. Not in the house!" and, ignoring their burdens, she shooed them in front of her to the trash cans. "Not in the house! Not, *not* in the bedrooms!" She pointed to the four large black trash bags that Mrs. Conroy had filled so long ago.

"Waste paper," she said indignantly. "Bones. Smelly old

books. Smelly old clothes. Not in the bedrooms! Not, *not* under my clean beds!"

"Well, it *was* all rubbish," said Big Grandma, who had once said she was all for second chances. "And if it was kept in trash bags, what was she supposed to think? What's over and done with is over and done with. Throw it away."

This holiday has changed Big Grandma, thought Ruth.

"Besides, I shall need the space going back," continued Big Grandma cheerfully.

"What for?"

"Wine, of course," said Big Grandma.

Perhaps she hasn't changed all that much, thought Ruth.

"You can bring back so much these days! Twenty-five years ago it was just a few bottles. So you see . . ."

"What?"

"Some things do get better," said Big Grandma.

Philippe isn't coming, thought Phoebe on Friday morning, and wondered if the others were thinking the same.

"It's gone all at once," said Ruth at breakfast time.

"What has?"

"This week in France. Tomorrow we'll be back in England."

"Thank goodness," said Naomi. "One more awful night!"

"There are no ghosts here," said Big Grandma firmly.

"There's something," said Naomi stubbornly.

"Well, I'll believe it when I see it," said Big Grandma. "Meanwhile, what about today? I shall be going on a wine hunt, but you really ought to see the market before you go.

The Friday market in the village, that is. Shellfish and cheeses and produce from the farms and lovely painted china. It's quite famous; people come from miles around to visit it, and you wanted to buy presents, didn't you?"

"Oh, yes," said Ruth. "For Mum and Dad."

"And Monsieur Carodoc," said Phoebe.

"And Joseck and Egg Yolk Wendy," added Naomi. "I'm beginning to quite like my hair!"

"Was it Egg Yolk Wendy who dyed your hair?" demanded Rachel and Phoebe in astonishment.

"Yes, and she was really frightened when she saw how it had turned out. I meant to send her a postcard to tell her to stop panicking but I forgot. I'll buy her something instead."

"And what about Philippe?" asked Rachel. "And Madame Carodoc?"

"She'll be so pleased we're going, she won't need a present," said Naomi.

"Get her some flowers," said Big Grandma.

There were loud sniffs around the breakfast table that showed what people thought of buying Madame Carodoc flowers. Nobody mentioned Philippe again.

"There's something strange about abroad," said Phoebe. "It's either very, very nice or very, very awful. It's never in between. I noticed it in Africa just the same."

They were standing in front of a fish stall, fantastic heaps scooped up and exposed to public view. The awful thing was that they were alive.

"Well, everything is alive until we eat it," pointed out Rachel.

On one marble slab was a particularly beautiful mosaic of fish, glistening with all the colors of water, sparkling with ice and embroidered with bright green parsley. Every now and then a fish would give a desperate heave. One, coral pink and dark-eyed, jumped and turned right over.

"*Celui-là!*" said a woman, pointing, and a moment later the pink fish was lifted from the ice and dropped onto the scales. Even Rachel averted her eyes.

The fish are beyond help, thought Ruth. They would never get back to the sea. The crabs groped and sidled, completely unaware of their fate, but the lobsters knew. The lobsters in the lobster basket were a simmering desire to escape. Because their claws were tied, their movement was slow and heavy, like movement in a dream, but nevertheless each continued its patient journey to the surface of the pile. One struggled and climbed its way right to the top, and was half over the rim before the stall-holder reached out an unconcerned hand and tapped it back in again.

"I'm buying that lobster," said Ruth, and, copying the pink fish woman, called, "*Celui-là!* pointing and holding out a handful of money.

"What are you going to do with it?" asked Phoebe.

"Put it back, of course," said Ruth.

The fish stall had been too much for Naomi. She had escaped and gone to look at the pets.

But are *they pets?* she wondered doubtfully. They certainly looked like pets, a crate of beautiful white rabbits and two little goats.

"Come on!" urged Ruth, arriving panting beside her.

"I've got this poor lobster that needs to go back to the sea. Let's go."

"In a minute," said Naomi. Money was being handed over. The two little goats were being bought and led away. In ones and twos the rabbits were beginning to disappear.

"Can they possibly be going to eat them *as well?*" wondered Naomi out loud.

"Of course not!"

"You'd think if they were choosing them for pets, they'd bring their children." Naomi continued her awful train of thought. "And there's something else . . ."

"What?" asked Ruth uneasily.

"They're choosing the fattest," said Naomi, and began to turn out her pockets.

"What are you doing?"

"Looking for money. We need another forty-five francs. See what you've got yourself."

"Nothing," said Ruth. "Phoebe?"

Phoebe handed over a couple of ten-franc pieces.

"Rachel?"

"But I need my money for Monsieur Carodoc's present. We haven't got him anything yet."

"Don't be silly!" said Naomi impatiently. "*These* can be Monsieur Carodoc's present! He can keep them in the orchard. Quick!"

Rachel sighed but handed over her cash just in time to save the last three rabbits.

"*Non! Non! Non!*" cried Naomi as they were put into three separate bags.

"English!" commented the stall-holder, but not un-kindly. "You want me to prepare them now?"

"Yes, please," said Naomi, watching with relief as he retrieved a rabbit from its bag. "A box with a bit of straw . . . *No!*"

The stall-holder, whistling cheerfully, had opened a large clasp knife and was heading with a rabbit in his hand to the back of his van. Phoebe grabbed his arm.

"Not prepare?" he asked, looking down at Phoebe.

"No, no," stammered Naomi. "I thought you meant . . ." She stopped because of course he hadn't meant what she thought he meant. How could she have been so stupid to have imagined that preparing the rabbits meant somehow explaining to them that they were sold . . . perhaps tidying their fur . . .

"Oh, please," interrupted Ruth. "Put them in a box. With airholes. So that we can carry them home."

To their enormous relief he did as he was asked.

"He was kind, really," said Rachel later.

He had been very kind. He had even rescued Ruth from the lobster, tying it up tight in a large damp sack.

"Keep him cool," he advised, "and he will be okay. Salt water, you know, as deep as you can. You understand?"

"Yes, yes," said Ruth. "Thank you very, very much."

"English!" he said again, smiling, and waved good-bye.

The rabbit box was very heavy and its occupants very excited. They hopped constantly from side to side and butted the lid with their heads. Naomi did not care. She had scraped up enough barn-wall French to get through a whole shopping trip, saved three lives, survived falling in love, and grown accustomed to blue hair. She hugged her bumping cargo and was happier than she'd been for weeks.

Chapter Ten

"FANCY RACHEL not wanting us to help her!"

"I know. Little beast! She said we wouldn't have a clue where to begin!"

"Actually, I wouldn't. Bad enough getting myself ready."

"I know, but she needn't have said so. Do you think Phoebe is going to turn up at the last minute?"

"Make a grand entrance?"

"Do you think Phoebe really is an international spy?"

Luckily for Ruth the tide was out. The triangular spit of tumbled rocks that jutted out into the sea was almost completely uncovered. Slipping and slithering she made her way between pools and boulders and sudden deep channels until she reached the outermost point. There at the edge the water was deep and clear.

"And it will be even deeper at high tide," she told the lobster as she untied his sack. "Anyway, it's the best I can do."

On the beach she had equipped herself with a large piece of broken razor shell. The elastic bands that closed the lobster's pincers had been fastened so tightly that they snapped apart at almost the first cut. Ruth hastily stepped back out of reach and at that moment the first wave of the incoming tide washed over the rock. When she looked down again the lobster was gone.

"You bought him *what?*" asked Big Grandma.

"Rabbits."

"*Rabbits?*"

"Three."

"Good grief! And where's Ruth?"

"She's putting a lobster back in the sea. That market was awful! *Awful!*"

"You bought me *what?*" asked Monsieur Carodoc.

"Rabbits. Three. For our good-bye present."

"Alive?"

"Yes, yes."

"Three alive rabbits?" Monsieur Carodoc repeated. "Three alive rabbits! Excuse me please!" And he walked suddenly around the corner.

The girls looked at each other in dismay but a moment later he was back, putting away a large white handkerchief.

"I hope you like rabbits," said Phoebe sternly.

"But of course! Very much indeed!"

"Anyway, you had to have them," said Naomi. "Otherwise they would have been sold to eat."

"Of course these are not to eat?"

"I believe," Big Grandma told him with some enjoyment, "you are expected to keep them forever."

"Or as long as possible?" asked Monsieur Carodoc hopefully, but was immediately squashed by Rachel.

"You can write and tell us how they are," she said. "That will be nice!"

"So it will," said Monsieur Carodoc.

"And send photographs," added Phoebe relentlessly. "So we can see they're all right."

"I don't know what Hélène, Madame Carodoc, will say."

"Oh!" exclaimed Ruth. "Madame Carodoc! We forgot her flowers!"

"She can share the rabbits," said Naomi, and nearly added, "Serve her right."

The rest of the day passed very, very quickly. There was no time to think of anything; they almost, but not quite, forgot to wait for Philippe.

The cottage, Big Grandma ordered, must be cleaned until it sparkled, everything except the bare essentials must be packed ready to be loaded into the car, and, as well as this, the rabbits' welfare had to be considered. This meant that Monsieur Carodoc must first be chivied into the immediate construction of a suitable hutch and run, and then kept under close supervision until it was finished. He showed no enthusiasm for rabbit hutch construction and had a tendency to wander off after Big Grandma whenever the guard was relaxed.

"Don't you like your lovely rabbits?" asked Rachel.

"Of course I like them," replied Monsieur Carodoc impatiently. "Of course, of course."

"I suppose they'll have forgotten us by the time we come back."

"Shall you come back?"

"Lots of times," said Rachel certainly. "When Philippe is better."

"Shall you come back?" Monsieur Carodoc asked Big Grandma. "Louise? Louise? Why don't you let the girls start packing the car and come and sit down for a while?"

"I prefer to pack it myself," said Big Grandma. "I shall do it last thing of all when everything else is sorted out. There are all those bottles to go in, and I cannot concentrate on driving if I am wondering all the time when they are going to start chinking."

"Louise, shall you come back?"

"I cannot bear chinking," said Big Grandma.

Late into the evening she was still packing and arranging.

"Strip your beds and bring everything down the moment you wake," she told them as she sent them up to bed. "We must make as early a start as possible."

"What, without any breakfast?" asked Rachel alarmed.

"Have I ever starved you yet?" demanded Big Grandma. "I'll have your breakfast waiting as soon as you all are ready and your beds are done. Now off you go upstairs."

"What will it be?"

"What will what be?"

"Breakfast."

"Goodness, Rachel!" exclaimed Big Grandma. "Would you like a menu? Breakfast will be breakfast! Coffee. Eggs. Rolls. If we have time, that is. Go to bed!"

"No *pain au chocolat?*"

"Bed!" ordered Big Grandma.

"But . . ."

"Very well. *Pain au chocolat* as well. Now, *good night!*"

"Good night," said Rachel happily.

Naomi was the only one who did not instantly fall asleep. Her mind had reached the state of tiredness where it could not rest, and her thoughts raced away from her like ribbons in the wind. The pink fish jumped again. Mr. Blyton-Jones snorted with laughter and flourished a book. Monsieur Carodoc said, "Louise, Louise." The rabbits were unbearably heavy and then all at once as light as air. It was terribly dark and she couldn't move and piles of lobsters slid over her head. Naomi, half-smothered in quilt, groped her way to the surface, rolled thankfully into the cool night air, and climbed out of bed for one last look at the apple orchard at night.

Less than a week had passed since they had arrived and yet the apple blossom was almost over. Naomi leaned out of the window watching as the petals drifted from the branches in the evening breeze and realized that it was not so late as she had supposed. Below her the ghost that only she believed in prowled between the trees, and Naomi, in a moment of clearheadedness, saw at last that it was no ghost at all, only Madame Carodoc walking in her apple orchard.

Of course it was Madame Carodoc, thought Naomi, both relieved and disappointed at the same time. *Of course, of course. And Big Grandma knew all the time. But what is she doing? She looks like she's looking for someone. Can't she see that there's nobody there?* And she stared and stared, growing more and more sleepy, until Madame Carodoc was lost among the shadows of the farthest trees.

Naomi was back in bed and almost asleep when she was suddenly struck by the most horrible thought.

The rabbits. The rabbits, who earlier in the evening had been ceremoniously installed in their hutch at the end of the orchard. Had it not been said that Madame Carodoc was to share them? And was that sensible? Was Madame Carodoc really likely to cherish rabbits supplied by her highly unwelcome guests and already predestined (to French minds, at least) for their ultimate fate in the cooking pot?

Without further thought, Naomi climbed out of bed, hitched herself over the windowsill, slid down the roof, and raced to the end of the garden to ascertain the fate of her precious rabbits.

Two minutes later she realized how silly she had been. Of course they were all right. There they were, all three, peacefully chewing carrots in the moonlight. Naomi turned and, as soundlessly as she could, began to make her way back to the cottage. Madame Carodoc, she was relieved to see, was nowhere in sight.

And a good thing, too! thought Naomi a moment later, because she had caught sight of the barn door standing wide open.

And after all Big Grandma said about not annoying her!
exclaimed Naomi to herself. She nobly crossed the grass to
slide the door shut before springing back past the Carodocs'
darkened windows and across the orchard to bed.

It seemed only a moment later that it was morning.

"Pain au chocolat!" shouted Rachel right in her ear. "I've
stripped my bed. Shall I do yours?"

Naomi groaned and then woke up with a jolt as her pillow was snatched from beneath her head.

"Go away!"

"It's morning!" Rachel announced. "It's nearly six
o'clock. I've woken Phoebe and tipped her out of bed . . ."
Rachel neatly removed Ruth's pillow and flipped away
Naomi's quilt. "Hurry up or there won't be time for breakfast."

"I bet you haven't even washed."

"What's the point?" asked Rachel cheerfully. "We're
going back to England today."

Naomi decided that perhaps there was some sense in
that and reached for her jeans. Ruth, still wrapped protec-
tively in her quilt, shuffled across the room to inspect the
morning from the window, and Rachel disappeared to
reawaken Phoebe, who had fallen asleep on the floor.

"Get off," said Phoebe. "Or I'll bite you."

"Big Grandma!" wailed Rachel down the stairs.
"Phoebe won't get up!"

There was no reply.

"And she says she's going to bite me!"

There was not even a clink of china from the kitchen.

"*Big Grandma!*" yelled Rachel.

There was no sound at all.

Her bed was unslept in and unstripped, her pajamas still under the pillow. There was no sign of breakfast in the kitchen.

"I hope she hasn't died in the Black Hole," said Phoebe, and they rushed outside and looked, but she hadn't.

"Well, she must have gone off somewhere," said Ruth.

"There would be footprints," said Phoebe, and they realized at once that this was true. The morning dew, so heavy that it made the orchard grass look almost gray, was completely undisturbed. Naomi could just trace a shadowy pattern that was her footprints from the night before. No one had walked to or from the cottage since.

"She *must* be in the house," said Naomi, and they searched it again.

"She's run away," said Phoebe at the end of the search. "Run off with Monsieur Carodoc. I thought she might."

"Don't be silly," said Ruth, but all the same she went outside and glanced uneasily across at the Carodocs' house.

"They're up," said Naomi, following her gaze. "Look! The chickens are out!"

Last thing every night, the girls had learned, the henhouse was fastened shut. "Against foxes," Monsieur Carodoc had explained.

"Perhaps Big Grandma let them out," suggested Rachel.

"Not unless she flew," pointed out Phoebe.

"I'm going over to the Carodocs'," announced Ruth, who had been feeling more and more uneasy. "Who'll come with me?"

"Me," said Phoebe at once. "I'm not staying here. Whatever happened to Big Grandma might happen to me! I just can't understand why we didn't hear any screams."

After this remark nobody felt much like being left behind. They set off together and as they grew closer noticed that the Carodocs' back door was standing wide open.

"I bet she's in there," said Naomi.

"I think there's something wrong," said Ruth, and at that moment a chicken sauntered out from the open door, glanced around in an aimless kind of way, and then, followed by two others, wandered back in again.

"Terribly wrong!" repeated Ruth, beginning to run. "Madame Carodoc would never, ever let a chicken into her house!"

Nobody came to meet them as they ran. Nobody answered their calls at the door, but when they peered inside there was a sudden flurry of wings and it was at once perfectly obvious that at least some of the chickens had spent a wild night in the house.

"There's nobody here at all," said Naomi.

"Perhaps they're upstairs. Call again."

They called again. On tiptoe they toured the ground-floor rooms, and then, with growing desperation, ventured upstairs.

"No one," said Ruth as they closed the final bedroom door.

"All dead," said Phoebe gloomily, "I expect."

"Shut up! It's not funny!"

"I never said it was. I don't like it up here."

"Come on back downstairs."

They came to a halt in front of the phone.

"We should call the police," said Ruth.

"We'll all be suspects," said Phoebe, "even if we do."

"Suspect what?" asked Rachel. "We haven't even had any breakfast yet."

"How can we call the police?" asked Naomi, ignoring them both and speaking to Ruth. "999 is for England. I bet it's something different in France."

"We could still try it."

"They'll only answer in French and then what will you do?"

"I think we ought to try it anyway," Ruth said, and tried it, and it did not work.

"I wish we knew how to call England. There's an international code . . ."

"At least we haven't found any blood yet," remarked Phoebe. "Of course, I suppose it might be under all the chicken mess . . ."

"Blood?" asked Rachel.

"Well, there's bound to be blood, unless they were strangled . . ."

"Phoebe, *shut up!*" shouted Ruth. "I can't think!"

"Why don't we call Philippe?" asked Rachel.

"Philippe?"

"I've got his number. It's in my crown."

"In your crown?" repeated Ruth and Naomi in astonishment. "Philippe's number is in your crown?"

"I'll show you," said Rachel proudly and, forgetting the possibility of being got by whatever got Big Grandma, shot off back to the house.

"Why ever have you got Philippe's telephone number in your crown?" demanded Ruth when she returned.

"It was his idea," Rachel explained. "He said, 'Where can I write it so you will not lose it . . .'"

"His telephone number?" asked Phoebe.

"And his address. So I would write to him. And then he said, 'Of course. In your crown.' Look! He put it all around the inside edge. And then his telephone number at the end. 'But if you were dialing from France,' he told me, 'you would skip the first part. The 00 33 . . .'" I'm sure he wouldn't mind."

"Mind?"

"Me telephoning. Even if he is ill."

"Wait a minute, Rachel!"

"It *is* an emergency," Rachel said, and picked up the receiver.

Chapter Eleven

"LOOK! RUTH, LOOK! By the door!"

"It isn't!"

"It is!"

"Crikey. You might be right!"

"Of course I'm right. Who else would wear dark glasses in church?"

"Can she see us? Wave! Wave!"

"It's all right. She's coming. Phoebe!"

"Phoebe!"

"We guessed you'd make a grand entrance! Shove up, Ruth, and make room."

"Phoebe, where *have* you been?"

"No good asking her that!"

"What will you do if it isn't Philippe who answers?" asked Phoebe. "What if one of his parents answers?"

"I shall just keep saying, 'Philippe!' until they fetch him."

"Is it ringing?"

"Yes."

"Is it still ringing?"

"Yes . . . Philippe?"

"Has somebody answered?"

"Shut up! Philippe . . . Philippe."

"Tell whoever it is to go and fetch him!"

"I don't know how. Philippe . . ."

"*Allez cherchez* Philippe!" said Ruth, her eyes screwed tight with the effort of producing so much French. "Say that."

"*S'il vous plaît*," added Naomi. "They're probably very polite, like Philippe. No point in making more enemies."

"All right," agreed Rachel, and breathing heavily into the receiver repeated, "*S'il vous plaît, allez cherchez* Philippe and *please* don't answer in French because I can't understand it."

"Rachel!"

"Someone said, 'Rachel,'" reported Rachel, turning away from the phone.

"Rachel? Is it Rachel?"

"I want to speak to Philippe, *s'il vous plaît*."

"You *are* speaking to Philippe, *s'il vous plaît*," replied a very familiar voice. "And how are you? And why have you not sent me any letters? I have written to you twice. What is your excuse? Have you lost your crown?"

"Of course not. I'm wearing it now."

"Does it still look nice? What else are you wearing?"

"Jeans. My blue sweatshirt and sneakers. New ones, you haven't seen them before . . ."

"Rachel!" interrupted Naomi. "Tell him what's happened!"

"Is that Naomi I hear?"

"Yes. Do you mind me calling?"

"Not at all, I am enchanted. Does Mrs. Conroy mind?"

"Mrs. Conroy?"

"Your mother."

"She doesn't know."

"Oh, Rachel!"

"She's in England."

"And you aren't?"

"*Tell him what's happened!*" hissed Naomi.

"Philippe?" began Rachel again.

"Still here."

"Naomi says I've got to tell you what's happened."

"Tell me, then."

"Well, we got up very early . . ."

"Earlier than this?"

"Oh, much. Hours. Because we wanted to have time for breakfast and we've got to catch the ferry."

"The ferry! Rachel, are you coming to France?"

"I can't tell you if you're going to keep on asking questions."

"Sorry."

"Early breakfast because we've got to catch the ferry. But when we went downstairs Big Grandma was gone."

"Gone?"

"She wasn't there."

"I am utterly confused."

"So we thought we'd better come across to the house."

"Which house?"

"This one. And it was full of chickens."

"Full of chickens?"

"Well, quite a lot. In the kitchen. And Big Grandma's pajamas haven't been slept in, and there's nobody here. And would Madame Carodoc really let chickens into her house?"

"Madame Carodoc?"

"Your *grandmother!*"

"Rachel, *where are you?*"

"Here," said Rachel patiently. "In Madame Carodoc's house. They're her chickens . . ."

"Give that phone to me and stop talking rubbish," ordered Naomi.

"No . . . Philippe?"

"I'm just coming," said Philippe, and hung up.

"There!" said Rachel triumphantly. "He's coming."

"You didn't tell him anything!"

"We can tell him when he gets here. Let's wait by the road."

After the Carodocs' dark little hall the morning sunshine seemed very bright and cheerful. At Rachel's suggestion, they collected the *pain au chocolat* and had a picnic beside the road. It was a great relief to get away from the chickens and the empty buildings and the silence.

"And the blood," said Phoebe with her mouth full.

"There *isn't* any blood," said Ruth. "It's almost like everything was quite all right. Perhaps they've just gone shopping or something."

The moment she said it she knew how stupid a suggestion it was. For a while they had almost been cheerful, but not now.

"They haven't gone shopping," said Naomi gloomily, and after that nobody said anything at all.

About ten minutes later Philippe arrived.

"Not quite on a white charger," said Naomi afterward, "but nearly!"

"A black motorbike!" said Rachel in an awestruck whisper.

For a minute or two they completely forgot the events of the morning because the sight of a contemporary on a motorbike was as cheering as the thought of Alan Adair in the butcher's shop had been dismal. The little wind of the future that earlier in the week had so coldly suggested their careers might be less than glittering blew suddenly warm.

"I shouldn't mind a motorbike," said Naomi, voicing all their thoughts.

"Is it yours?" asked Phoebe.

"Borrowed," said Philippe climbing stiffly to the ground and beginning to remove his helmet. "Well, stolen from a friend but I will give it back."

"Won't he mind?"

"Forget the bike. *Why didn't you tell me you were here?*"

They gaped at him in astonishment.

"Didn't you know?"

"Do you not think that I would have come if I had known?" demanded Philippe so indignantly that they had nothing to say in reply. "Why are you here and why so secret?"

"It wasn't meant to be secret," protested the girls.

"I am terribly upset," Philippe continued, looking terribly cheerful.

"Well, so were we."

"I wasn't," said Phoebe.

"Tell me all that has happened!"

So, with many interruptions and exclamations, the story was told of Big Grandma's sudden decision to take them on holiday, and the strange week in France where Monsieur Carodoc had been so welcoming and Madame Carodoc so cross.

"Poor *Grand-mère!*" said Philippe, beginning to laugh. "But I am not surprised!"

"Why not?"

"Your grandmother and my grandfather are too much good friends for my poor *Grand-mère,*" explained Philippe. "It is a joke in my family, *Grand-père* and his English lady! So my grandmother would certainly not be happy to see her again; or you either, since I talked of you so much."

"Did you?"

"Naturally!"

"But last Sunday when Madame Carodoc went to visit you we were already here. Didn't she mention us at all?"

"She mentioned you all the time because I told her all about my visit to your home and she was not pleased."

"Not pleased about what?"

"That I had stayed with you and liked you all so much."

"Did you really?"

"Yes, even despite the mayonnaise. And naturally I told her of Rachel's kind proposal. She was not pleased at all! 'That terrible family!' she said. 'First Charles and now Philippe! Julie, you should not encourage him!'"

"Who's Julie?" interrupted Phoebe.

"My mother. You might see her soon. I left a message for her to tell her I was coming here."

"I hope she's not going to hate us as well."

"Of course not! She thinks *Grand-père* and his English lady very funny and she likes your mother. She said, 'Can Philippe and the girls not be friends?' And my grandmother said, 'Certainly not! No more visits! No more letters! No more talk of them at all!' She was very indignant, and no wonder, with you all living in the cottage even as she spoke! But we didn't know that."

"She told Monsieur Carodoc that you had flu and we thought that was why you didn't come."

"You did not," said Philippe. "You thought I was a treacherous friend!"

"*I* didn't!" protested Rachel.

"And you thought, If he will not come, then we will not ask him," continued Philippe remorselessly. "And of course my grandmother would never tell me you were here, but why did *Grand-père* not say a word?"

"We wouldn't let him," admitted Ruth.

"*Grand-mère* is right," said Philippe, beginning to laugh. "Proud scheming English, she says, and so you are! Except Rachel, of course; she does not scheme! I do like your hair, Naomi!"

"That's one of the reasons we came," Rachel told him. "We were going to blame Naomi's hair on the French."

"Charming!"

"And of course it was partly to cure Ruth of the family failing as well."

"Shut up, Rachel!"

"No, do not shut up!" said Philippe. "Tell me more! I remember the family failing very well. Falling in love. Not a good thing! Phoebe's dead-letter box. Is that not correct?"

"You *can* read English!" exclaimed Phoebe. "You are a pig, Philippe!"

"Of course I am," agreed Philippe cheerfully. "And why else did you come?"

"Cover for Big Grandma," said Phoebe, and then all at once they remembered why they had summoned Philippe in the first place.

"Big Grandma!" exclaimed Ruth. "We forgot!"

"She's lost," Rachel told Philippe. "And so are Monsieur and Madame Carodoc. And we've got to catch the ferry this morning and we've had hardly any breakfast and their house is full of chickens."

"*What?*"

"Like I told you on the telephone."

"I couldn't think what you were talking about."

"Come and see," said Naomi urgently.

"Is it a joke?" asked Philippe, beginning to follow her toward the house.

"No, no! They are really lost . . ."

"Lost or dead," put in Phoebe. "Or both."

"We ought to call the police," said Ruth. "We ought to have done it ages ago but we didn't know how."

"Strangled," explained Phoebe. "No blood, no screams."

"All three?" asked Philippe cheerfully.

"I suppose so. Madame Carodoc's gone, too, otherwise

it might just have been Big Grandma and your grandfather."

"Run away together, you mean?"

"No, dead. And Madame Carodoc the strangler. But she'd never have left the door open. I don't see what's so funny."

"Stop making me laugh and listen," said Philippe.

"What to? Where are you going? Come back!"

"I'm just going to see what is happening in the barn."

"In the barn?"

"Can you not hear? Stop talking and listen!"

They stood still and listened, and, sure enough, faint shrieks and banging noises were coming from the barn.

It was Philippe who released the captives, and he did it alone.

"Cowards!" said Big Grandma as she raced the laden car across the Brittany countryside.

"We couldn't bear to look."

"Whatever did you expect to see? Blood on the barn floor? No, don't answer! I must concentrate on the road. I've got to drive fast!"

Everything had been fast, from the moment the barn door had opened.

"No time to talk!" Big Grandma had cried as she shot into the daylight. "Explanations later! Pack! Pack! Pack!"

"What about breakfast?"

"Breakfast!" snorted Big Grandma.

Amazingly enough, though, breakfast appeared.

"*Vite! Vite!*" called Madame Carodoc as she emerged from her chickeny kitchen laden with ham rolls and hot coffee. "Hurry! Hurry! Eat at once! Philippe, come and serve your friends! Julie!"

Right in the middle of the race to hurl everything into the car and eat Madame Carodoc's rolls without choking, Philippe's mother arrived, scolding Philippe, teasing the Carodocs, and hugging the girls.

"Promise me you will come back," she urged. "You must stay with us next time. All four!"

"Soon?" asked Rachel.

"Very soon! We must be very good friends. Now tell me how the grandparents came to be shut up in the barn!"

"Julie, it was not funny!" said Monsieur Carodoc.

"I think it was perfect," said Philippe's mother. "Perfect! Only it ought really to have happened twenty-five years ago!"

"Big Grandma," said Rachel. "What did you do in there all night?"

"Talked," said Big Grandma.

"Aren't you mad with Naomi?"

"How was I to know there was anyone in the barn?" demanded Naomi.

"Quite," agreed Big Grandma. "Of course I'm not angry! Am I ever unreasonable?"

"But why were you in there in the first place?"

"I was packing the car. Monsieur Carodoc was helping me, or trying to. Actually he was getting in the way . . . And Madame Carodoc had been out to see your blessed rabbits and she popped in on her way back . . ."

"To see what you were up to," interrupted Naomi. "Like she's been doing all week."

"Naomi!"

"I thought she was a ghost. Phoebe thought she was a spy. That was her face at the window that night."

There was a long silence.

"There have been a lot of misunderstandings," said Big Grandma eventually. "Too many. Julie was quite right when she said we should have been shut up in the barn together twenty-five years ago!"

"So are you all friends now?"

"I really *must* concentrate on the road!"

All at once it seemed, the rolling Brittany countryside had been left behind them and they were speeding down the long straight French roads that led to the ferry port. Everyone else on the road seemed to be hurrying, too.

"French drivers!" exclaimed Big Grandma crossly. "They're never happy unless they're overtaking. Here's another blasted roundabout coming up! Nobody talk!"

French roundabouts were having the same effect on Ruth that she had noticed on the journey down. They were conjuring up the school bus driver, and this time Ruth understood why. *Tenez le droit!* read the signs at every roundabout.

"It feels so unnatural," grumbled Big Grandma. "*Tenez le droit*, indeed!"

"I knew I'd seen it somewhere before!" exclaimed Ruth. "That's what he's got tattooed on his arm!"

"Who? What?" demanded Naomi.

"The school bus driver. '*Tenez le droit*,' like it says on the roundabouts. That's what he's got up his arm."

"The school bus driver," explained Naomi to Big Grandma, "is another of Ruth's family failings."

"Pleasant?" asked Big Grandma.

"Not at all. And he calls her the dead-hedgehog girl."

"He calls me what?"

"Spare your sister's feelings if you can, Naomi," said Big Grandma. "None of us choose to fall in love."

"It's all right," Ruth told them. "I've fallen out."

"Just like that? You fortunate child. How many more to go now?"

"He was the last," said Ruth.

"I hope you didn't forget your seasickness tablets," said Big Grandma as they lined up for the ferry. "I meant to remind you, but it slipped my mind in all the rush."

"Madame Carodoc reminded us."

"Good heavens!"

"I remember now," remarked Ruth, still thinking of her bus driver. "Me and Wendy making out what it said just before Philippe went back. And I thought perhaps it was a quotation. Something out of *King Arthur*. It sounds like it should be: '*Tenez le droit.*'"

"It isn't, though," said Naomi. "French road sign, that's all. How can you possibly be in love with someone who calls you the dead-hedgehog girl and has French road signs tattooed on his arms?"

"You just can't," said Ruth thankfully.

"Well, perhaps this holiday hasn't been a complete waste of time after all," said Big Grandma. "Naomi is reconciled to her hair . . ."

"Actually a bluer blue would be better," said Naomi. "And perhaps a bit shorter . . ."

". . . and Rachel has forced someone to agree to marry her."

"Not forced!" protested Rachel.

". . . and how many people have you fallen out of love with this past week, Ruth?"

"Four," said Ruth.

"Not bad going at all! And what about you, Phoebe?"

Phoebe was remembering a conversation she had overheard that morning between Rachel and Philippe's mother.

"Has Philippe told you I'm going to marry him?" Rachel had asked.

"Dozens of times!" his mother had replied. *Dozens!* thought Phoebe, and sighed.

"I suppose I shall still have to be an international spy," she replied.

Once onboard the ferry Big Grandma found herself a sunny corner out of the wind, flopped down with a sigh of relief, and said, "Now we can stop."

"Aren't we going to have anything to eat?" asked Rachel, but there was no reply.

"It's all nearly finished," said Ruth.

"School on Monday," agreed Naomi.

School, thought Ruth. Well, that would be all right. Philippe was safely over and done with and out of the way. The bus driver was at last nothing more alarming than a bus driver again. Fat-Slob-and-One-Leg had appropriated Mr. Blyton-Jones (for what he was worth). There was no Mr. Rochester to keep her awake at night anymore. She was a vegetarian and Alan Adair had chosen to be a butcher. So that was that.

"Never again!" she said joyfully. "No more falling in love for me!"

"Nor me," agreed Naomi.

"What's that?" asked Big Grandma, opening her eyes for a moment. "Are you saying you are cured?"

"I'm not," said Rachel. "And I don't want to be. Nobody I fell in love with ever said they weren't in love with me!"

"Oh, take her away!" groaned Big Grandma. "Go and see if you can see England yet. Carry her off and feed her. Throw her overboard if necessary; anything, only buzz off the lot of you and leave me in peace!"

"Are you going to sleep?"

"Perhaps."

Only Phoebe, lingering after the others had gone, saw that Big Grandma did not go to sleep. She stayed wide awake, staring back and back at the line of blue cloud where France had been.

They think they've been cured, Phoebe thought, looking down at her sisters as they made their way across the lower deck and she remembered: Madame Carodoc kissed Big Grandma good-bye. She kissed her *hard.* Four times, twice on each cheek. They sounded like smacks.

There is no cure, thought Phoebe.

"Thank goodness that's over! Now for the party!"

"Look at them smirking!"

"Good old Rachel, she got him at last!"

"He didn't take much getting. He was hooked from the start."

"Did you see Big Grandma and Madame Carodoc fall into each other's arms?"

"Yes, right at 'Speak now or forever hold your peace!' I think they were laughing."

"I suppose we'd better go and congratulate the bride!"

DATE DUE